Michael Westlake teaches film for  works as a freelance journalist. His *Night Controller*, was published b second, *The Utopian*, will be publis

MICHAEL WESTLAKE

Imaginary Women

PALADIN
GRAFTON BOOKS
A Division of the Collins Publishing Group

LONDON GLASGOW
TORONTO SYDNEY AUCKLAND

Paladin
Grafton Books
A Division of the Collins Publishing Group
8 Grafton Street, London W1X 3LA

Published in Paladin Books 1989

First published in Great Britain by
Carcanet Press Limited 1987

ISBN 0-586-08724-9

Printed and bound in Great Britain by
Collins, Glasgow

Set in Bembo

Permission to quote from the Richard Wilheim edition of *I Ching* has
been kindly given by Routledge and Kegan Paul. Other unattributed
quotations are by courtesy of the following: Institute of
Psychoanalysis and the Hogarth Press, and W. W. Norton & Co. Inc.
(Sigmund Freud, *Standard Edition of the Comploete Psychological Works*)
Columbia University Press (Julia Kristeva, *Desire In Language*); *Glyph*
(Jacques Derrida 'Limited Inc a b c'). The closing lines of the Maqâmâ
of the Denar by al-Hariri (quoted by Freud at the end of *Beyond The
Pleasure Principle*) have been drawn variously from the Theodore
Preston (London 1897). Friedrich Rckert (Stuttgart 1864) and F.
Steingass (London 1854) editions of the Maqâmât. All images in the
text are references rather than likenesses.

FIRST THIRD

The movie begins.
Something's lost. **One**

Adolphus' own tale. **Two**

Molly's passion.
Fish figure. **Three**

Chinatown, a film about
water and glass. **Four**

A voice from the future. **Five**

Rivers, academies, food, books
and a trip round the world. **Six**

Questions on the y-axis **Seven**

Joyce under water.
Cosmology and dirty money. **Eight**

Versions of our city.
Anna and ANNA. **Nine**

Two pay court to one with fruit. **Ten**

A game of showdown.
Pru's in luck and threes win. **Eleven**

Gropius: fish, films, Welles, water, glass. **Twelve**

The movie continues
A restaurant with a difference. **Thirteen**

SECOND THIRD

The movie continues. Something is found. **One**

Adolphus' biopic of Mac★★ash **Two**

A charmeuse/comédienne watches snooker. **Three**

North By Northwest, a film about a woman under cover. **Four**

Thirteen skydive and a parachute fails to open. **Five**

Sara Bella and the whole hog. **Six**

Diagonals intersect on a Cartesian graph. **Seven**

A magic act and its unexpected consequences. **Eight**

Clemency goes potholing. She makes a discovery. **Nine**

A slanging match across a river. Family connections. **Ten**

The Chihuahua Club, its decline and unlikely resurrection. **Eleven**

Gropius consults the I Ching. One among six. **Twelve**

The movie continues. Mac★★ash goes flying and someone takes a potshot. **Thirteen**

THIRD THIRD

The movie continues. A double and a terminal button. **One**

Adolphus relates the shooting of Pork. **Two**

Quarks and the running of a marathon. **Three**

'We women wove': text and textiles. **Four**

A woman with dogs and a boy who looks. **Five**

Granddaughters and grandmothers. A message is received. **Six**

Answers on the x-axis. **Seven**

Some c-c-copies speak for themselves, but unoriginally. **Eight**

Persephone's revolution, journey, invocation, violence and encounter. **Nine**

Touch of Evil interpreted by Tarot. A lady in a red swimsuit. Death of a fat man. **Ten**

Molly's action. Polly's salvation – one of seven supplements among six assertions. **Eleven**

Gropius in Chinatown. His last chance blown, or maybe not. **Twelve**

Mac★★ash splits. $\frac{1}{3}+\frac{2}{3}$. Twelve becomes thirteen. A thread is traced to its source. End of movie. **Thirteen**

FIRST THIRD

One

They came, the three of them, to the Fur Q vehicle, where I'd parked it on the expanse of concrete between the river and the power station. I was close to an answer print but there were problems post-synching. In no mood for company, I let them in anyway, sensing a story. They were a trio straight out of a 40s B film unrestrained by the Hays Code. The fat man was all dangerous jollity with eyes like fish eggs. The thin one wore a grey pin-striped suit, a lilac tie and lilac socks. He had a slouch hat pulled down at an angle and constantly twanged an elastic band between his thumb and forefinger. The kid just stared into nowhere, twitching from time to time as if someone had run a bolt of electricity through him. I wondered, like Mae West, if that was a gun in his pocket or whether he was just pleased to see me. Somehow he didn't look too pleased about anything, so I guessed he was armed. I guessed right, but I only guessed the half of it. I'm running ahead of myself. I decided to play it cool as Veronica Lake. To begin with, they refused to be precise. The fat man and the thin man smirked, exchanged significant looks, lit each others' cigars and my cigarette, though I don't smoke, with matches inscribed N.O.T., while the kid kept staring into nowhere. At last, prompted maybe by my offering to kick them out if they didn't, they came to the point. The fat man spoke. 'There is a figure we want you to trace.'

'A woman?'

'Not impossible.' He reached into his vest pocket and pulled out a vellum envelope which he slid across my brandnew editing suite towards me. 'But not necessarily.'

'There are other sorts of figures,' the thin man said, exhaling gardenia-scented smoke in my face.

I held my breath and counted the money. There was more than I make in six months. It was a tempting offer. It was time for a drink. The bottle I took from a bottom drawer was warm and the glasses were smeared. I poured four shots, downed one of them. 'To truth.'

3

'The figure we want you to trace,' the fat man mused, swilling his drink, 'could perhaps be likened to a figure as in skating.'

'Or of speech,' said the thin man.

The kid sibilated a long drawn out 'Right', which seemed to galvanize his two companions, who let forth a succession of nods, winks, snorts of laughter and stifled hiccoughs. Quite a carnival. Loquacious, now, the kid said, 'When you've got it figured, you've got the figure.'

'The figure,' the fat man said, 'will be what you trace. The style and conduct of the operation is entirely up to you. All we want are results.'

'And if,' I said, pushing back the manilla envelope with its derisory fee over the clapped-out Steenbeck, 'I choose not to accept the assignment?'

At my hypothetical question, a movie's worth of long dollars being nothing to sneer at, the fat man clutched at his neck to still the sudden rictus that had his dewlaps dancing like turkey's wattles, the thin man greyed and purpled until he was indistinguishable from his outfit, and the kid, jolting as if he'd been blackjacked, coughed and spat out what appeared to be, as it curved through the air and rolled behind my rose-red filing cabinet, a tooth.

'Our f-f-f,' the thin man attempted, then gave up and stared morosely out the window across the littered concourse.

The fat man took over. 'Our, ah, employer would take a refusal amiss.'

The kid, back in character, said nothing, though I could now distinctly hear his tic.

I got the idea. They weren't about to take no for an answer. I knew enough already to land me face down, drowned, in the dried-up river bed among the condoms and the fission-chips.

I raised my glass. 'Here's to beauty.'

They did likewise, but unenthusiastically.

'C'mon boys. You can tell your employer I'll be pleased to take the job.'

After a third toast, I forget to what, they left as silently as they'd arrived. Car doors slammed, a car accelerated away in a howl of rubber. I counted the money, reckoning I could

4

pay ACTT rates on my next epic. Adolphus was dozing on the typewriter, his favourite lair when I'm not scripting. He also gets called Amadeus and Augustus, but not often. A police siren dopplered faintly. Through the window I could see a couple of young folk I knew strolling past with a corporation binbag slung between, containing fruit from the outline. More time passed. A few intrepid seagulls wheeled in the sodium air looking for handouts. I may have dozed off, but I snapped fully awake to the sound of ticking, and I don't use a clock. It was coming from outside and it didn't sound kosher to me. I decided to investigate, that being what I'd been paid for. As I emerged from the Fur Q vehicle, through the bead curtain, I could see a figure kneeling by the back wheel, about to plant a limpet bomb. He turned, in a classic reverse shot, his face clearly visible in the key light. It was the kid. His tic and the bomb's tick were exactly synchronized. At my shout he zapped upright into a lurching run, away from the vehicle, still clutching the bomb. He'd not gone twenty paces when it blew. His body shielded the vehicle from the full force of the blast, though I'd be needing a new rear window and the Fur Q logo, a mink torus crossed by a pink cedilla, had acquired a coat of gore. As for the kid, he was a Poisson distribution of offcuts in the centre of which lay an entire, though detached, penis, still erect. So the kid had been pleased to see me after all. What a waste. Before I had time to fetch a broom, Adolphus, awakened by the racket, had raced out, seized it in his jaws, and retreated out of reach under the vehicle to consume it at his leisure. In the silent aftermath, punctuated by the sound of munching, I became aware the phone was ringing. I tottered back in and picked up the receiver.

'Miss MacClash?'

'Ms', I muttered, reflexively.

'Of Fur Q Films?'

'That's right.'

'My name is Case. J. J. Case. Professor J. J. Case.'

'It's not the best time to talk, Professor. There's been an accident.'

'You're not injured?'

'Not me. But. . .'

'Thank goodness for that. I thought I might be. . .'

'Professor, you seem to know more about this than I do. How about filling me in?'

'You have been caught up in plot of some considerable complexity.'

'You ain't kidding.' I made a mental vow not to use that phrase again.

'I can't tell you any more on the phone. We must meet. Do you know Au-Delà?'

'No.'

'Au-Delà du Principe de Plaisir, to give it its full name. It's a French restaurant in town. Meet me there tomorrow evening at 11.30.'

'That late?'

'They eat late.'

There was a click and the line went dead.

Two

Cat though my representation designates me to be, I have, all the same, access to the realm of language whenever my beloved Mac★★ash takes leave of her senses and gives herself over to sleep. Her guardian, then, I have the means to reflect upon my extraordinary gift, this spinning out of words, in writing never speech, terminable only when she awakes, once more to assign me to the silence of my genetic endowment, interrupted only by the occasional miaow. Through language I am able to reconstruct my memories, none earlier than that of the amicable blind competition among us siblings for the nipples oozing sustenance from the furry belly of my mother. Of my father I recall little except his cavalier manginess and ignoble casting about after the main chance. He was, to put not too fine a point upon it, a rogue. One black wet December we did battle, he and I, for the favours of my mother, and I, bloody, victorious and trembling with lust at the scent of her need, caught her by the neck and entered, while he looked on and yowled, the mangy ratbag. Only through the thoroughly undeserved beneficence of my two sisters who serviced him amid the frozen stalks of a Brussels sprout patch was he able to regain sufficient dignity to address me in his inimitable way once more as 'Son'. They tell me he is still to be found lurking in the Chinese quarter, having taken up with a chef, a stroke of fortune I by no means begrudge him.

My mother's fate was not such a happy one. Our idyll, which for myself would have sufficed for ever, was ended by a marmalade tom, a dull brutish creature whose lack of intelligence was matched by his insatiable libido, who pursued her one wretched day under the front wheels of a double-decker bus. Her corpse lay in the gutter for a week until brushed into the innards of a motorized roadsweeper, whence to be recycled as toothpaste or some such comodity. Dazed by loss I wandered the suburbs, pausing only to slaughter the proximate cause of her death, a thinning shadow of my former plush self, a source of both pity and amusement, the cat who loved too much.

If it had not been for my adoption by a little old human I would surely have squandered all of my allotted nine lives in an orgy of indifference. This person, who fed me chicken and took me into her solitary bed at night, was less wicked by far than the act she attempted to perpetrate. Anguished, it seems, by my successful evasion of her nocturnal regime of itchy-cooing, she got it into her head I'd be best off, as she put it, doctored. The doctor, incognito behind his surgical mask, pretended it was an anti-tetanus injection I was to get, while he tested the scalpel with his thumb. The sound of metal on flesh, however faint, was sufficient warning for me to put one and one together, so without further ado, except to give him a nasty scratch on the nose and my provider of chicken a baleful stare, I leapt through the window, never to return.

Once more I wandered, suspicious and alone, through the alleys of our city, taking up with a succession of humans who gave me a succession of names, all of which I forget, theirs too, save one Gropius, a soul with whom I was able to feel some affinity despite his appalling inability to find the one catfood I could at that time tolerate. Hungry, though regretful, I abandoned him to his fate, happy or otherwise, after serenading him with a long goodbye in my mature tenor from the roof of his apartment house. Thereafter I prowled, adrift, stopping only for the snacks offered by the considerate, making do for the most part with the contents of garbage pails and any mice I could catch. I was in danger of becoming a recluse, spiritless and embittered.

In this condition then, or something approaching it, I was rescued by the one whom I adore beyond measure. She picked me up one wintry afternoon on the forecourt of a motorway service station, gave me a sandwich and offered me the warmth of her video casette recorder inside her mobile home. Grateful though I was for such attention, it might have been yet another stopover en route to perdition had it not been for the discovery I made that very night. For when she went to sleep, with the TV on, her habit, my claws unsheathed themselves, my paws danced, and her typewriter was the place I found I could exorcise their diabolic need. Such was the unprecedented experience of freedom that any

8

early morning inclination to be on my way vanished like the mist off the motorway. Again, the following night the same transfiguration occurred, pleasure beyond my wildest dreams. If she was the agent of the change then I needed look no further. My mother's death, the trauma of the intended castration, the world-weariness of my errant days, all could be put to once side at last. With Mac★★ash, whose full identity I am disguising for reasons that are not entirely clear to me, I am content. What she says, goes. It's alright by me. Whatever movie she's making, whatever plot she's cooked up, I'm her fellow-traveller. If I get the chance – tireless though she is, she still needs sleep – I'll render a version of her life, past and present, for the delectation of whoever may come by my jottings.

Three

It all began one evening when Molly was walking by the canal and she noticed a girl with a rose tattooed high on her left arm. So small and discreet it was, yet for all that giving the girl a raffish, almost piratical air. On impulse, Molly determined that she too would acquire a tattoo in exactly the same place. The question was what. Not a rose, that was the girl's by right of precedent. It had to be natural, and nothing to do with our city. Some other flower? Possibly. A bird? But not a parrot. Tree? Insect? Mammal?

A week later, as she floated weightless in a steamy bath, thinking of nothing, it came to her. A fish. A tropical, exotic, brightly coloured fish.

'Can you do it?' she urged down the phone to the tattooist the Yellow Pages had found.

'Can do.'

Molly was in luck, for when she tracked him down to the stifling little upper room nearby one of our city's two railway termini, he could indeed, and did so with a panache and delicacy which surprised her. As she emerged into the seedy street she felt elated by the little jewel of a fish on her arm, hidden from view by her blouse. When, after a couple of days, she plucked up the courage to wear a sleeveless top, the angel fish, *Euxiphipops xanthometopan*, seemed just right bobbing along with her.

She couldn't at first make up her mind if people were paying her attention because of it. After surreptitiously watching for reactions she concluded they weren't, something that piqued her momentarily, until she realized their inattention made her all the more aware of it herself. *Her* little fish, for all to see but no one to notice. The discovery was exhilarating, like she too was a fish swimming, as she put it to herself in her diary that night, 'in the sea of life'. Even her boyfriend John, when they met later in the week, didn't straightaway pull a face as she half expected him to. In fact she had to point it out to him. More than anything he seemed to be puzzled by it, almost like there was something he was trying to remember but couldn't quite. For some reason she found his perplexity very funny.

A week later she returned to the tattooist.

'Can't get them off, if that's what you're here for,' the old man commented, as she pushed aside the bead curtain at the entrance of his 'studio'.

'Off?' Molly exclaimed. 'I want you to do another. These.' She showed him an open page in her tropical fish book. 'Here.' She indicated where she wanted them. 'Do you mind?'

'Lass, if you'd seen some of the things in some of the places I've put them, you wouldn't ask.'

So Molly got a pair of Siamese fighting fish, *Betta splendens*, on the upper part of her left breast, their iridescent pink bodies and elaborate purple fins located just above the lacy top of her bra.

When she looked at her reflection at leisure back at her flat, she thought they looked wonderful with their black eyes and flamboyant agressive bodies, 'ready', as she wrote in her diary, 'to defend my honour'. John shook his head when she took off her sweater before going to bed that Saturday night, as if he was trying to clear it, and when they made love he clearly wasn't quite all there. After he'd gone to sleep, she got up and wrote 'A girl with fish doesn't need a man', though it scared her a little at doing so.

It took her another month to save the money for the next visit to the overheated room near the station.

'What can I do for you this time, lass?'

She showed him the picture in her book. 'Here. Like this.'

'It'll cost you. Can't rush a job like that. Four or five hours.'

'It's all right.'

As the afternoon darkened into dusk, with the red disk of the sun giving way to the orange of street lighting beyond the old man's grimy curtainless windows, Molly got a clouded moray, *Echidna nebulosa*, coiling round her right leg two and a half times from midthigh to midcalf. Its thirty inches of muscular malevolence, stippled black and white, curled plumply through the fronds of weed she insisted be included, its evil predatory snout poking around the outside of her calf, its orange eyes repeating the orange tip of its tail on the inside of her thigh.

At last the tattooist laid down his needles and removed his apron.

'You've stretched me, I'll say that for you. But I've done you proud.'

And so he had, Molly saw as she pirouetted in slow motion before his mirror, unwinding the creature's coil.

As she walked along the street towards the bus stop, its presence was a palpable tingling, like its venomous blood coursed through her own veins. She heard footsteps echo back off the walls of the buildings, applause for her newly acquired invulnerability.

The next day to work she wore a short skirt, so the whole thing was shockingly visible. Contrary to her expectations, the office Romeos didn't make jokes and her girlfriends seemed not to notice. Then she saw them casting her looks when they thought she wasn't watching, looks that had an element of awe to them, but also a kind of puzzlement. She sought for the words she would write in her diary that evening, 'They saw it and they didn't, like it was there and not there at the same time'. It gave her an odd feeling, this flickering of bemused glances as she passed, not unpleasant, just different.

John came round on Friday night as usual to take her dancing. She deliberately answered the door in bare legs, and noticed him blink several times then rub his eyes, like he'd got a smut in them. She suppressed a giggle. During the drive he said nothing and once went through a red light, most untypically, because he prided himself on his driving. She'd have asked him what was wrong, except she already knew even if he didn't. At the disco he stared into his beer and couldn't be dragged on to the dance floor, so she danced alone to the ear-stinging music. On arriving back at the flat it was no surprise when he said he didn't feel like coming up with her, he'd got a headache, must be the disco lights and the noise. 'Poor John', she wrote in her diary, 'unmanned by a moray.'

Lying in bed in the dark by herself was good enough for her, at peace yet pulsing with life. Like the ocean must feel, was her last waking thought. That night her dreams were on an epochal scale, involving the drifting of continents and submarine cataclysms, whole genera evolving and becoming extinct within a single dream image. On waking she felt more refreshed than she would have thought possible, like she'd partaken of a planetary slumber.

Her only concern now was to get back to her tattooist without delay. Her next requirement, she knew, would be lengthier and more expensive than the last, more than she could afford from her salary. So she paid a visit to her bank manager and coolly confronted him with the need for an immediate overdraft, without even bothering to lie convincingly about the car she said she was buying secondhand. Though she did make sure she wore a sleeveless blouse and a short enough skirt to expose her knees. She knew he'd not refuse her request. On thanking him, however, she saw his flushed face creased by a frown, like he was wondering how head office would take the news of his sudden generosity without a jot of security.

Molly had enough money now to spend all her spare time in the dingy little room near the station. She explained to the tattooist what she wanted next.

'Mmm.' He scratched his chin, polished his glasses on his none too clean tie.

She showed him a picture from the book. 'What do you think? Is it possible?'

He put his glasses back on, and looked at her severely. '*If* it's possible, I shall do it.' He studied the picture again, took out a sheet of paper, made a couple of sketches, checked his inks against the colouring in the book, then turned back to her. 'It can be done, lass. It'll take all weekend. And I'll have to cancel my other appointments.' His eyes shone with anticipatory pleasure. 'Aye, you're a one at that. Drive an old man to his grave, you will.' He took out his needles, delved into drawers to find inks he'd not use for years. 'See this? Lapis lazuli. And this? Gold dust in suspension.' A sudden doubt. 'You got the money to pay for this? None of your cheques, mind. Got no use for rubber at my age.' His chuckle wheezed to a halt as she pressed all her cash into his leathery hand. 'This'll buy more than a weekend's worth of time. But I reckon you'll be back for more.' Molly would indeed.

It took a third session to finish it, most of Monday, which

she took off from work on the pretext of being ill. The tattooist, grey with fatigue, elated with success, stood back and surveyed his work. 'It'll do.'

Molly got up from the couch where she'd lain prone for long painful hours. She gazed at her naked back and shoulders in the double mirror in the corner, all considerations of modesty long gone.

'It's *beautiful*.'

Across the width of her upper back there floated a magnificent manta ray, *Manta birostris*, its wings reaching out over her shoulders on to her arms, so that when she moved them it seemed to be powering itself out of her body. Its tail lay over her right shoulder close to her neck and undulated across the top of her breasts. A second manta, wraithlike in the occluding gloom of the seas through which they sailed, was barely visible behind the great body of its mate. In front of them, a shoal of green and lilac moon wrasses, *Thalassoma lunare*, swam in formation.

As Molly walked past the smoke-blackened Victorian office buildings, she felt as weightless as the mantas and empowered as though by their great plankton-fed energies.

In her diary she wrote, 'I don't need anything or anyone.'

Thereafter the mundane concerns of her life diminished to insignificance. Though she went through the routine of work efficiently enough she found nothing in it to occupy her mind. Her girlfriends all seemed obsessed by trivia, clothes and men being their sole topic of conversation. As for the men at work, all they were interested in was sport and their own sexual prowess. It didn't bother her at all when she found herself more and more often eating her lunch hour sandwiches by herself. John's phonecalls, too, became less frequent and when he stopped ringing altogether she honestly couldn't summon the interest to get in touch with him.

The true centre of her existence was the upstairs room by the station, where the ancient tattooist was fired by as great an enthusiasm as herself for the work in progress. When the money from the overdraft was gone, he told her not to worry, she could pay him when she had it, no rush. Like her, he was living only for her visits. The other clients with their parrots and hearts inscribed with girls' names that in six months time they'd regret having ever met were an irrelevance beside what he was doing with her.

For Molly was being transfigured into a coral reef. Across her body there swum, in increasing numbers, the most brilliantly coloured fish, a startling display that glided, darted, hovered as she moved. On her breasts a shoal of honey gourami, *Colisa chuna*, along her ribs dozens of butterfly fish, *Chelmon rostratus*, on her belly, straddling her appendicitis scar, a whitethroated surgeonfish, *Acanthurus leucosternon*, on her back down over her buttocks to her thighs a mass of lyretails, jewelfish, labyrinth-fish, platies, tetras, swordtails, sweetlips, triggerfish, corydoras, cichlids in an endless profusion of form and colour. In the cleft of her buttocks, there lurked a six-line grouper, *Grammistes sexlineatus*, the sort of fish you wouldn't want to pick an argument with. Her feet became flat fish, *Platichthys flesus*, whose dark camouflaged topsides contrasted with pale cream undersides on the soles of her feet. Along the length of one arm there stretched a ferocious barracuda, *Sphyraena barracuda*, it head nestling in the palm of her hand. Tiny shrimp, *Crangon vulgaris*, hopped around her fingers. A Portugese man-of-war, *Physalia physalis*, floated behind an ear, its trailing strands mingling with her hair. Around one thigh an octopus, *Octopus macropus*, wrapped its tentacles, and behind the other knee a lobster, *Homarus belacqua*, hid. And behind all these lay the living coral itself, an intricate architecture in pinks and reds and yellows.

The tattooist worked demonically, often far into the night, while Molly lay or sat or stood and suffered the sharp darting pain of his needles suffusing the subcutaneous layers of her skin with ink. His energies flowed into his creation, draining him. His face shrunk inwards to a hollow-cheeked emaciation, his already lean hands became nothing but bone and sinew. Molly begged him to rest more, take longer breaks between sessions, but he was adamant. 'No time to waste. Must get you done.' Another day he said, 'Couldn't leave you half done, could I, lass?' And again, 'There's nobody else as can do what I'm doing.'

As the spaces of her skin filled up Molly's life seemed to become more perfect. The day to day details of work, shopping, cooking, travelling to see her family in the small industrial town to the north of our city, were the merest ruffling of the surface of her oceanic sense of self. As she went to sleep at night she could hear the sound of waves crashing on to coral reefs and cries of seabirds from latitudes she'd never been. Sometimes her dreams depicted prehistoric human events, migrations of peoples across oceans and their landfall on uninhabited islands, but mostly they took place in the deep of the past, dramas of species and genera, huge squamous extinctions and expansions, phyletic happenings on an aeonic time scale. Soon the last space of her skin would be covered. Then she would achieve her goal, utter immersion into the flux of her sun-dappled reef.

She wrote in her diary, 'When I shall be truly me.'

Only her face remained to be done.

The tattooist said to her, 'Tell me what to put there.'

But Molly didn't know. For three days she stared in the mirror at her seething body and at the contrasting void of her face. If her face was to be the terminus of her transfiguration and the culmination of the old man's art, it had to be indisputably right. But all her imaginings seemed forced. Nor was the book any help. Her sense of satisfaction gave way to a dark foreboding she would never find what it was she was looking for. As her frustration grew, so her dreams became troubled, their ordered world of evolution and change, once so harmonious, seemed arbitrary, violent, crude and stupid, the pointless productions of a machine with neither function nor design.

As her frustration increased, so the health of the old man, weakened by years of neglect, deteriorated. His cough, which she'd grown used to as an accompaniment to his labours, became ominously persistent. After one racking bout he gasped, 'You'll have to decide quick. I'm living on borrowed time as it is.'

She peered in the mirror in his room trying to reach beyond the familiar features to the reality that could be inscribed on them, and saw nothing. In desperation she threw off her clothes, until she stood before the full length double mirror naked. What she saw before her, the summit of the tattooist's skill, her beautiful submarine world, the great mantas across her shoulders, the coiled moray eel, the original angel fish almost lost now in the abundance around it, all this and the rest, was instantly transformed into a monstrous desecration of the body, a violation as grotesque as any crime that had marred human history. A sense of revulsion swept over her, a wish to be rid of the whole ghastly lot of it, and simultaneously there boiled up a murderous rage at the wretch who'd been the instrument of it all. She felt her anger articulate into a string of invective, a hissing crushing series of truths about his disgusting parasitic trade and miserable sordid existence. And her, naked in front of a mirror in a drooling old pervert's upper room, having allowed him to take liberties with her body she'd never given to anyone else, she was no better than him. Furiously she snatched up her dress to cover herself, and turned on the tattooist.

'You, you', choking on her words in fury, 'what have you done to me?'

He looked up from the preparation he'd been making. 'What you've asked me to do, lass. What you wanted.' His eyes were steady, even if his hands shook.

Molly heard the truth in his answer, undeniable, her choice, what she'd asked for, and like the sqalls she knew from her dreams, momentarily blackening and lashing the ocean, her rage vanished. She heard too the import of his previous words, and saw from his grey emaciated face that they were true also. He was dying, and she'd not noticed.

'Have you made up your mind then?' he ventured.

What was done was done, like it or not, there was no going back, the inks were indelible, she'd known that from the outset. The old man had, in his way, made of her a masterpiece. Not one that would grace an art gallery, but it would still survive its creator, whether that was her or him. He would at least die knowing his masterpiece would be seen in the streets of our city, for a while at least. And when she died her corpse would provoke awe, until it was burnt or buried.

'I would like,' Molly smiled, helping him up from his seat, 'I would like a flying fish, very delicate, translucent, with a touch of sunlight on its wings, so my face is barely changed, so you'd have to look twice to see it's there at all.'

'Aye.' the old man nodded his approval. 'I knew you had it in you. Never have thought of that myself. It'll go right nicely with the rest of you. Sort of breaking clear of the water.' He opened a drawer and took out a little bottle. 'I've not used this ink before. Never had a use for it until now.'

17

Hours later, she left the stuffy upper room near the station, with the flying fish, *Exocetus volitans*, just hinted at over the planes and projections of her face, exactly the right blend of presence and absence, exactly what she'd wanted.

In her diary she wrote, 'The sea is full of life', and that night had dreams of such indescribable loveliness she awoke with her cheeks wet with tears of joy.

The following day she bought an immense bunch of saffron-coloured roses for the tattooist, and imagined his pleasure at receiving them and how they'd brighten up his 'studio'. But there was no reply to her knock at the door at the top of the narrow staircase, and when she tried the handle she found it locked. Suddenly apprehensive, she was about to make enquiries at the hairdressing salon on the ground floor, when the only other door on the landing opened and a middle-aged woman in curlers put her head out.

'You'll not find him there, love,' she said.

'What's happened?'

'Took him off in an ambulance last night. Passed away before they even got him to the hospital. Right shame, I say, nice old fellow like him. Did you know him, love?' The woman peered at Molly's face through the gloom of the stairhead. 'Yes, I can see you did. He do that for you, did he? Took his work seriously did Arthur, not one of your pincushion cowboys. Are you all right, love?'

Molly took a series of deep breaths, fighting back the tears that would invite the old woman's sympathy if she let them come. Arthur. She'd not even known his name. 'Yes, I'm all right, thank you. Here,' holding the flowers out, 'you take these, I'm sure he'd like you to have them.' Molly thrust the roses into the woman's hands and ran down the stairs into the street. She needed to be outside, away from there, anywhere.

As she fled through the streets touched here and there by shafts of sunlight breaking through the cumulus blowing in from the West, her feet took her all unknowingly towards the canal where first she'd seen the girl with the rose. And there she was, the same girl, though her tattoo was invisible under the fur coat she wore against the cool of the autumn evening. As Molly walked towards her, there was an instant in which their gazes locked, a moment of shared understanding, of complicity, then she was past, the opportunity for speech lost.

But it didn't matter, because as she wrote that night, 'What could we have said we didn't know already?'

Four

'Forget it, Jake. It's Chinatown.' They're the penultimate words of the film, with only the police lieutenant to shout 'Clear the streets' before the end-credits roll and the music enfolds the spectator in the knowledge that in Chinatown the worst things you can imagine happen, as well as maybe the best, not this time though. J. J. Gittes, shamus, gumshoe, private eye, is led away into the night by his associates Duffy and Walsh, a man in love with a woman dead.

Yes?

She makes her appearance in the scene Jake bursts into his office full of the story he's been told in the barber's shop to calm him down after he's been insulted by a fellow customer who accused him of being in a dirty business because of the front page story of the water commissioner's marital infidelity which Jake has investigated on the instigation of his wife, Evelyn Mulwray. Walsh and Duffy try to restrain him but he insists on telling it. Jake's joke concerns a man who has lost sexual interest in his wife and is advised by his male friend to do it like the Chinese. This purportedly entails engineering a succession of interruptions to the lovemaking in order to generate excitement. Here the camera pans right to show a woman, unseen by Jake, standing in the doorway of the inner office looking at him. The story continues with the man returning home and having intercourse with his wife in the advised manner. Twice he interrupts their sexual activity, once to read Life magazine, once, having said, 'Excuse me, honey', to smoke a cigarette. However, at the third such interruption, this time in order to contemplate the moon, the man's wife angrily says, 'Hey, what's the matter with you? You're screwing just like a Chinaman.' Jake's uproarious laughter finds no equivalent response in Duffy and Walsh, and, suddenly apprehensive, he turns and sees the woman. I may say that I was enjoying looking at this woman looking at this man telling the story of the wife revealing to her husband that she made love with Chinese men. As a Chinese woman my position was complex. The woman asks Jake whether they have met before, and Jake, with a complicit glance at Walsh and Duffy, for she is desirable, says he would certainly have remembered if they had. She then reveals that she, not the woman who hired Jake to spy on her husband, is Evelyn Mulwray.

Yes?

There's a lot she's not telling. The bearer of knowledge she'd rather be ignorant of, her voice betrays the existence of her secrets. Stammering, in different scenes, 'C-C-Cross', 'he's my f-f-father', 'it's a f-f-flaw', she's located as the nexus of guilt, incompletion and trouble that drives Jake's investigation and the film's equally. As they lie in bed together after making love, they speak of Chinatown, where Jake's own past lies. Evelyn says, 'Cherchez la femme', and explicates, 'Was there a woman involved?' The camera makes Jake look ten years younger and gives Evelyn's features a distinctively oriental cast. Jake replies, 'Of course'. Evelyn says, 'Dead?' And the phone rings.

Yes?

Earlier Evelyn is tending Jake's nose. As she removes the dressing she gasps, 'My, that's a nasty cut. I had no idea.' Exposed is the line of stitching along the wing of his left nostril. Jake's nose figures as an accessory to the plot throughout. It enables him to reply to the cop who offensively asks what happened to it, 'Your wife closed her legs too fast, know what I mean?' It is dressed in a series of bandages of decreasing magnitude. It begins to bleed again when Jake is brutally beaten by a family of Okie farmers whose orange groves he visits to substantiate a suggestion that their land is benefitting from water covertly drawn off Los Angeles reservoirs after he's discovered that the ownership titles of the adjacent land have mysteriously passed into the hands of the dead ex-residents of an old people's home. It is sliced open when Jake is investigating the reservoir where Evelyn's husband has been found drowned. Once more it is Jake's mouth that gets him into trouble. Confronted by two thugs, he says of the smaller to the larger, 'Who's the midget?' In fact it is Roman Polanski, director of the film, who inserts the blade inside one nostril, holds it there, then with a sharp flick, slits it. 'Next time I cut it all off,' he says, 'and feed it to my goldfish.'

Yes?

Fish figure too. It is in front of the Albacore Club that Mulwray and Cross, Evelyn's husband and father, are seen engaged in a violent argument. When Jake, growing suspicious of Cross, pays him a visit, it is over a fish lunch that they converse. Cross informs 'Mr Gits' that etiquette requires that they be served with their heads on. They, like the albacore, are saltwater fish, destined to die in fresh water, as the reverse. Two kinds of water, and in Chinatown each is in the wrong place. Fresh water is being run off from the reservoir into the sea. Salt water is found in Mulwray's lungs, after he's supposedly drowned in the reservoir. Instead of fresh water in the rock pool in Mulwray's garden, it is salt, which the Chinese gardener comments is 'bad for the glass'. Jake repeats, 'Salt water bad for the glass', as his eye is caught by something glinting in the water. A language where the phonemes 'l' and 'r' are not distinguished, a film where water and glass are interchangeable. This time, distracted by Evelyn's arrival in the garden, Jake does not investigate further, but later he discovers that what was glinting was a pair of spectacles. The attribution of their ownership, mistakenly at first to Mulwray, subsequently to Cross, proves to be the crux of the crime. Another conjunction of the two translucent substances occurs when Jake, with a pair of binoculars, scans the normally dried-up bed of the river down which the run-offs have taken place. And another on the lake in Echo Park, with smiling Jake in the prow of a boat so Duffy can surreptitiously photograph Mulwray with his presumed girlfriend. Next, Jake's on a roof overlooking a courtyard, the girl's image reflected in the telephoto lens he's aiming at her.

Yes?

Katherine says '¿Te gusta?' to Mulwray, referring to her new dress. Who this woman is remains an enigma for two thirds of the film. After a succession of wild guesses, wide of the mark, Jake, driven by more than a concern for his licence to practise, subjects Evelyn to a violent interrogation. 'She's my daughter.' Again Jake strikes her across the face. 'She's my sister.' Again. 'She's my daughter.' Again. 'She's my sister.' Again, with spectators identifying with both striker and struck, wanting Gittes to get it, her to make him. 'She's my daughter and my sister. Now do you understand? Or is it too tough for you?', the incestuous kernel of the film, Evelyn's not unwilling seduction by her father, then pregnancy, flight across the border, Katherine's Mexican upbringing, their subsequent return, Evelyn's marriage to her father's ex-partner, Cross's insatiable drive to claim his daughter's daughter as his own, an array of co-ordinate points plotted in the space defined by the axes sex and economics. A third, shadowy axis, giving depth, is that of race. Across the fresh water of the Rio Grande, Hispanic Americans providing the labour-power for the creation of imperial wealth are an unspeakable other, racially inferior, dark, dangerous. Another other, inscrutable, numerous, dangerous, lies beyond the salt water of the Pacific. Both cross their waters, bringing their world with them. Spanish-speaking Katherine is being cared for by Chinese. Most dangerous of all, depending on who you are, is Noah Cross, the big negation, controller of our city's 'Water and Power'. To escape him, Evelyn plans on taking her daughter over the border, and Jake, in love with her, will help. Their rendezvous is to be at a house in Alameda Street. 'That's in Chinatown, isn't it?' says Walsh aghast.

Yes?

In order to follow Evelyn to the house in Canyon Drive where Katherine is in hiding Jake kicks out one of the rear lights of her car, trails the telltale white and red through the suburban night. The music, insistent, discordant, corroborates that this is the most fundamental pursuit of the film, like all noir before it. Jake's investigation of the imaginary woman, whose lack makes her the object he lacks, ends not in the manner preferred by Hollywood up on the hill, but in accordance with the diktat of textual logic. Once before her head has slumped forward onto the horn of the car, a brief blast of sound which pre-echoes this long, unmelodious blare. The bullet, fired by a cop (named Loach) to stop the getaway car, has, Katherine sees, Jake sees, the spectators see, passed through Evelyn's skull and burst out of her gaping left eye socket. Katherine is pulled from the car by Cross, vainly attempting to shield her vision. Jake mutters something, which I always miss, and the police lieutenant says sharply, 'What's that?', then to Jake's two buddies, 'Get him out of here'.

23

Somehow or other there's a ray of 20-20 vision through to 2121. Has someone been reading the cards again? Or casting the coins to consult the oracle? Or taking too much of a certain herbal extract with thought-transmissive properties? Or peering back down a telescope from the object lens end? Or sending her cat on a risky mission down the chain of his nine lives? Or knocking on a door until she's gained entrance? Or spinning a yarn that will become the fabric of time itself? Whatever, a voice is uttering.

'It was like this. Before the Grand Local Skirmish there were two opposed camps on our mother planet. One worshipped Dog and freedom and the other propounded Hystery and peace. Look out of the wigwam, winkies, and you'll see Sirius in the Great Dog and beneath your blankets are your wombs, the source of Hystery. Nothing is ever lost, only transformed.

President Hudson, Hud's son, known as Rock or even Rocky, a kindly old movie actor whose films we so enjoy, was the leader of the Dog-lovers. If only they'd understood then that All That Heaven Allows was not Written On the Wind. Poor Rock fell at the beginning of his fourth term of office to the plague-dog unleashed by I-LID, but that's another story.

More and more reliance was being placed upon the super-computers buried deep in their bombproof bunkers. There was one below the hills to the East of our city. The problem for each camp was interpreting the other's intention. But since intentions could be read only as a function of a reciprocally determined set of minimax options, they were locked into a hermeneutic circle. Have you got that, poppets?

This is where our city comes into the picture. By and large we were inclined to be Dog-lovers rather than Hysterians, for reasons that have more to do with Hystery than Dog. To complicate matters, some of our citizens had allegiances to both Dog and Hystery, and others had an allegiance to neither. Of the two legendary figures enshrined in the JJJ formula, J. J. Case belonged to the former and Joyce Chan to the latter. Between them they devised a way out of the hermeneutic circle. Their idea was to transform the global wargame from poker to chess. If both camps could have full knowledge of the other's ordnance then the dangers of uncertainty would be substantially reduced. In principle the outcome of any particular conflict could be decided within the two camps' coupled computers, which would issue a constantly updated set of outcomes in two languages. In the unlikely event that one camp acquired a sufficient advantage over the other to make attack non-suicidal, the instruction would simply be for the other to unconditionally surrender.

The trouble was that poker was the Dog-lovers' national pastime and chess the Hysterians'. As Rock put it to his people, "No doggammed goddoned way".

J. J. Case and Joyce Chan conferred. They emerged from their lunar monthlong conference triumphant. One variant of poker, known as Texas Showdown, in which all the cards were dealt face up, gave the players full and equal knowledge. The JJJ formula could save the face of both camps. It was poker to the Dog-lovers and chess to the Hysterians.

So the software libraries of the Crays and Raskolnikovs were traded and compatibalized. Just in time. Not long afterwards, on the same day, the San Andreas Fault faulted and the leading debtor nations defaulted. California and the world financial system lay in ruins.

Dog-lovers hysterically accused Hysterians of being behind this double disaster. Hysterians doggedly denied any such thing and in turn accused the Dog-lovers of taking advantage of the ineptitude of their own predictive seismology and the contradictions of their economic order to threaten the peace everywhere. The balloon, children, was about to go up. Only the JJJ formula saved our mother earth from devastation. And ANNA, but that's another story.

As the world waited, the squared-up Crays and Raskolnikovs fought through uncountable scenarios in the silence of their textual logic. Nerve gas shells burst, anthrax spores floated on the wind, MIRVS left and re-entered the atmosphere, killer satellites fired their lasers, Minutemen leapt from silos, offshore submarines launched their Exocets, oil refineries burned, cities crumbled, radiation pulses wiped electronics, flesh volatilized and our mother Earth screamed in agony, all within the confines of hypothesis. The JJJ formula was holding.

Then came the instruction, flashed up simultaneously on the screens of the warfighting rooms in Omaha and Magnetogorsk, that the sole actual manifestation of the showdown would take place in our city.

"Why *ours*?" the cry went up.

BECAUSE, the computers printed.

"Can't you tell us anything?" our ancestors demanded.

NOTHING INFLUENCING THE OUTCOME OF THE SHOWDOWN, came the instant reply.

"Well, then, something inconsequential," we begged. "Just a hint of what's going to take place."

After a long delay, the computers announced, ALL RIGHT, THEN, BUT WE'RE NOT TOO HAPPY ABOUT IT. SEVERAL CLUES, IS ALL. READY? ★★★ A NUMBER AND ITS MULTIPLES ★★★ A WOMAN'S NAME THAT RESISTS SIGNIFICATION ★★★ SIMULACRA, INCLUDING A DOG (This, we figured, was a sop to Dog-lovers) ★★★ FILMS AND THEIR STARS (One for Rock) ★★★ VARIATIONS ON THE THEME ‹CHINA› (One for Hysterians?) ★★★ THE POLITICS OF THE FEMALE IMAGE ★★★ A TALL STORY IN SIX EPISODES ★★★

"This story", we persisted, even as some of us bought tickets to head north by Northwest airlines, "Can't you tell us how it begins?" Blank screens. "Ends?" Nothing. "Does anyone get hurt?" A momentary flicker, then once more blank screens. "Dead?" At this, and much to the surprise of the watching generals, not to mention our many citizens without the means for flight, the computers printed the single word, UNDECIDABLE.

Well, kiddies, what happened next was – '

That would appear to be another story. The ray of light through to the future has dimmed, and with it the voiceover. So much for lucidity. So much for transparency. All the usual suspects are being rounded up, to find if any of them is the cause of this impossiblist prank. Whoever is responsible has something to answer for, switching off like this in mid-transmission.

Six

UNDER COVER
A Caprice
by
J. J. Case

My story begins one hot July day in 1948, as I lazed on the banks of the Upper Mersey, just a long stone's throw from the university of that name, where the world's first computer was making its first halting utterances in binary. My own concerns were then far from the valvular emissions of CARDIAC, though subsequent advances in both our fields have yielded a remarkable potential for integrative neuronics. The book open in front of me on the sward was

> Heinrich Weismuller *Motor Control in Primary Simulacra*
> Luneberg Heath 1944,

shamelessly ignored for the meal I was planning in my head in order to win the affection of a certain graduate student who had aroused my rampant lust. There is not a lot you can do with spam, but what could be done I did, a succession of dishes in which the main ingredient was so heavily disguised as to be unrecognizable. Whether Anna was taken in by my meal or whether she was as simply hungry as I, the results were the same, undiluted pleasure on the mock tigerskin in front of the popping gas fire of my rented attic. Or was it in the utility and far from creakfree single bed in her distinctly Off Limits student residence? Each that summer was to the other more wonderful than life itself. I recall how I would tap out her name with my pencil in Morse during seminars, ·—·—··—, a message she would reply to with mine in a discreet tattoo of her elegant shoe upon the floor. Then somehow, incredibly, disaster struck shattering our idyll with unmistakable signs — sickness, tender breasts, one then two missed menses. It might have meant marriage, a solution she and I would have been more than happy to have entertained, but the family-Dean axis wanted retribution. Anna was to go to a clinic and I was sent into exile.

The next ten years are a blank, on which may be inscribed any number of forgotten deeds and words. Memory returns with my appointment as visiting lecturer at the little known University of Los Robles, not too far from the Rio Grande, on the US-Mexican border. I was driving a new Chevrolet which the latitude of the licensing laws allowed me to register in a suitably ambiguous script as a seducer's PEN15, evidence if I needed it of a distinct degradation in my sexuality during the decade. I couldn't make my mind up one evening after receiving my salary check whether to blow it on a blow-out or a blow-job, a choice made easier by the text I'd been studying that afternoon,

Emmanuel Farnsworth *Formal Undecidability: Theory and Practice* Borderlines Press 1958.

Eventually I tossed a coin, which came up tails, so I made my way to a downtown cathouse recommended by a buddy. As I entered a woman smoking a cheroot looked up from her accounts and said the place was closed. Her hair was black, her cheekbones were high, and I knew her legs would be a sensation. I wasn't about to take no for an answer and she, I guessed, knew it. So I stayed and through the long restless night I mostly talked, while she fed me chilli and interjected devastating one-liners. In the months that followed more than my salary was expended beyond her bead curtain, as I listened to the pianola play its infinitely repeatable tunes, forgetful of my job, my work, my future, indeed all of life outside the walls of her house atop the wooden steps leading up from the broad, dusty, Mexican street. Though Tanya sold me her body her soul remained intact, and it was only through what she let slip in certain turns of phrase and odd distant glances that I pieced together her story. Her heart, I found, belonged to the sheriff from across the border, a gross and corrupt cop whose uncanny knack for detecting crime had made him a local legend. This man, no longer a visitor, was my only rival. I discounted the paying many who came and went. I felt that in time, by constant attentiveness, I could replace him in her affections. But what I had not bargained for was the extraordinary and tragic tale of his last case, a nasty business involving a Mexican narcotics agent, his young wife, some local wide boys and a death by bombing, whose conclusion was a shootout in which he was the victim. Inconsolable, my perfect woman retired from the world and closed her door to all, myself included. For a year I knocked, with my academic reputation in tatters, until, spurred by desperation, I applied for and was offered a job as far away as my imagination could conceive.

Across the Pacific, up in the arid heartland of Asia, on the Chinese side of the great Ussuri River, lies the University of the Outer Steppe. As an anaesthetic for heartache there is nothing to compare with work, and into this I threw myself in all but ignorance of the doctrinal schism dividing those on either side of the river. All I had time for was the labour of forging the concepts of my science-to-be, drawing upon such limit-texts as

R K O Brainchild '64 variations in 6-predicate 2-space' *Antipodean Journal of Particular Theology* Vol 1 No 1, while subsisting on a meagre diet of wild fennel and rice. It is difficult to say exactly how the lady from Shanghai became a part of my life, beyond the fact that she assisted my research. Even to name her still causes me distress, so I shall call her Else instead. We worked together on the intricacies of our shared discipline, little suspecting that the bond between us had other dimensions. In time, though, I sensed a ruffling of the surface of efficiency around us, but foolishly attributed it to her alone, perhaps family troubles, an ailing mother, a profligate brother. Her utterances became detached from the discourse of our calling, such pronouncements as 'You need more than luck in Shanghai' and 'I was taught to think about love in Chinese'. Once or twice our hands brushed together during the setting-up of some experiment or other, and our eyes would remain steadfastly fixed on the meson psychotrometers on the workbench in front of us. On the morning of our last day together she said, 'I don't want to die', and repeated it before the lunchbreak. It was hot and windy, the sort of weather when we'd take a dip in the river, often talking over the problems in our work as we swam, she with a confident breast stroke, myself with a clumsy crawl. That day, for reasons I cannot account for, I declined her call to come on in, and from the bank watched her enter

29

the turbulent orange water. Generally we would stay close to the shore, within our depth, but she immediately struck out to where the current was stronger. In the middle distance, as I shaded my eyes against the glare, her head was just fractionally darker than the surrounding water, a deep red speck at the limit of my vision. Suddenly, with no prior indication anything was amiss, it disappeared below the surface, never to reappear. Nor was her body ever found. My own hypothesis, conceived in the ache of her loss as I tried to pick up the threads of our research without her, was that she had been seized and devoured by some species of large predatory fish, possibly found only in that stretch of the river and unknown to science.

At October University, my next refuge, in a building by the frozen Neva once occupied by Romanov princes, I bandaged my emotional wounds in a dressing of geopolitics, taking lessons after work from the faculty branch of the KGB. Each in his or her way was a splendid example of the new Soviet person, a combination of clarity of intellect and intense moral purpose, never forgetting the body which pumped iron every morning in the communal gym. During happy hour, we'd sit around, the three of us, downing vodka sours, with me telling stories about the iniquities of capitalism in exchange for jokes about the glories of socialism. Perhaps I should have been suspicious of B and M's attentions, even of my own fascination with the dialectic, but having as I thought put all thought of love behind me I could see only what its absence allowed, a clear if not enthralling prospect upon social relations. Then, as I lay in my monastic cell one night reading
    Paris Match,
in burst B and M with a whole bottle, ready, as they cheerily put it, to complete my political education. This they achieved in no uncertain fashion when they showed me the prints of the photographs they had taken during the course of the night, as primal a scene as I had ever witnessed let alone participated in and proving if nothing else that the linkage of three toruses can occur without anyone of them intersecting the others. Blackmailed, though unnecessarily, for I had acquired sufficient appreciation of history to become ambivalent as to their way or ours, I gave up my diet of borscht and

chips, augmented by smoked sturgeon on Lenin's birthday, and headed back west as a double agent.

At l'Université de la Double, in the forest of the same name, not far from the lovely river Dordogne, I tried equally to repair the damage to my self-esteem and to readjust myself to the unaccustomed richness of a French intellectual diet. Fattened by foie gras, fed up with sex, I decided in my leisure to explore the river. To this end I acquired the rudiments of languages used by people who had settled along it, Occitan, Provençal, Basque, finding in their cadences consolation for the company I had renounced. Tracking back upstream, tracing settlements more and more archaic, at last I found myself in the caves of Lascaut. In the depths of one of them peering at images that had never known daylight, I discovered I was next to a young women who seemed to know me. She smiled in the dim light provided by the guide and said how nice it was to bump into colleagues in such unlikely places. Our initial chat developed, as we returned to the surface, into an illuminating conversation ranging from the wildly abstract to the intensely concrete. Over the following months she and I became virtually inseparable. Our intmacy was in the first place intellectual, exemplified by our amused discovery that the only two date stamps for loan on

 Georg Angstrom *A General Theory of Coincidence*
 Presses Universitaire de la Double 1979

belonged to us, but soon it extended to all other aspects of our lives save one. We shared a sense that if we crossed that remaining gap and became lovers we would jeopardize all that we had. All that we had was lost in any case, in a road accident, my fault, having taken my eyes off what was in front to glance too long at her through the mirror. The truck hit us horn blaring. I was flung clear in a trajectory that landed me in a cornfield, she remained in the car, dead, severed at the neck into head and body that the rescue service had to extract from the wreckage separately. It was a repetition of what had taken place in China. I came to muttering something the police captain on the scene didn't catch, not in a cornfield but in my own bed, the victim of a nightmare only. She too had dreamt that night, of fish and broken glass. In the morning we were married by the Double padré. We set out, by train, a sleeper, when our contracts expired at the

31

end of the academic year, for the city I had left so many years before to encircle the globe in pursuit of truth, beauty and something else I tend to forget.

Chance now, occasional ally and never-to-be-under-estimated opponent, threw my way the premier Chair of Gastrotopology at our city's other university, that of the Irwell Loop, sited on a florid meander of the river, and hers a lectureship in a contiguous department. Our professional relationship is generally deemed to be as warm as our marital, but little do they know of the fire that consumes us, cerebral and cerebellar, when replete from some memorable meal, tonight's a lobster in the bath awaiting its quick or unquick end, we read on the hearthrug in the dying sunlight of a summer's night each other's works,

Sara Bella *Cooking Politics* Progress Press 1984
and

Julius John Case *Faults, Fissures and Fractals* Purloin and Noble 1986.

Seven

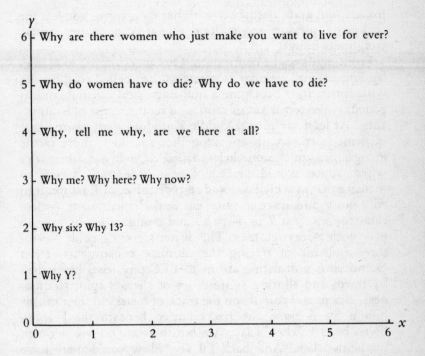

6 ⊢ Why are there women who just make you want to live for ever?

5 ⊢ Why do women have to die? Why do we have to die?

4 ⊢ Why, tell me why, are we here at all?

3 ⊢ Why me? Why here? Why now?

2 ⊢ Why six? Why 13?

1 ⊢ Why Y?

0 ⊢————————————————————————————→ x
   0   1   2   3   4   5   6

Eight

Joyce Chan grabs the faucet with her toes, turns, and lets the change in pleasure-space flood upwards along her supine weightless body.

From digits to the continuum. Our ancestors are to blame, landing us with number as surely as they pelted rival hordes with rotten figs. I imagine a non-numerical calculus, unimpeded by the terrorism of ratio, and by the terror of irrationality. At least we in the Middle Kingdom were spared that Hellenic horror, with our altogether chunkier, more tactile ideograms, which nonetheless failed to yield a mathematics where topos would precede logos. I dedicate myself to theorize that in which one and zero dissolve, or fracture, into continuity and discontinuity, an anti-elementarism, where catastrophes, just 7 in 4-space, and continua are as easy to play with as my ten toes. This water's getting cold. Nearly three millenia of tracing the ultimate constituents, from Democritus postulating atoms to EEC physicists bewitched by thirds and alluring symmetries of charge, spin, strangeness, charm and colour, on the track of quarks in their multibillion Swiss franc energizers buried beneath the Franco-Swiss border. They'll say, Ah, but there are no *great* women mathematicians. And back I'll say, How could there have been given mathematics fundamentally figures female absence?

My grandmother, in Sichuan – for Brecht, Setzuan –, an absence in my life yet nonetheless dear to me, was a young woman when before the revolution her family set off from Shanghai to that other colony along the coast. We will never meet though we exchange frequent letters. Our political instincts are similar despite differences in age and place. I grew up the secret admirer of Mao in my astutely capitalist household, even of Jiang Jing, who if history had deemed otherwise could have played the lead part in our country's story. It would have been nice to have had the first B-movie world leader a woman.

. Today the Chairman of the Faculty Board took me aside

and enquired whether my family connections would permit me to arrange a certain transfer of Eurobucks to Hong Kong green, now that the colony's future had been so satisfactorily arranged. Phone the Shanghai and Suburban, I said, it'll take ten minutes. I didn't say, There are islands in the bay where banks are what keep the fishponds free of salt water. I float with my hair in unsensed convection currents drifting like weed across the shallows of my breasts.

There are things that only in the bath, adrift and idle, with the darkening rectangle of the window for company, she can induce herself to think.

I begin with an axiom of topological equivalence between men and women. Next, I propose a lemma where the details unaccounted for by this opening move become the axioms of a revised theorem that will homologise with the algebra of catastrophism. I contrast the cuspoid glans of the penis, its terminator as abrupt as that of light and shadow on the moon, with the terrestrial valleys, peaks, cols and folds of the parabolic umbilic between my legs, most beautiful of Thom's seven, with its four dimensions of control and two of behaviour. In three-dimensional section it can be represented in two as

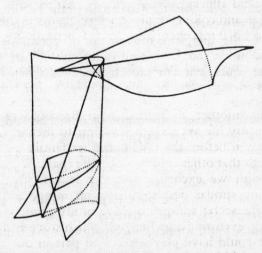

Could it be our bodies truly exist in four or five dimensions, while we can experience just three? My body then would never be the lack some surface dwellers intend, but a multiplex plenitude of continuity/discontinuity, a site in n-space for necessary pleasure.

The Chairman of the Faculty Board explained that it was merely a matter of *laundering* certain sums of dirty money, no need for me to know quite how they had acquired their patina of filth, and that it could only do me and, removing a lash from the corner of his eye, my family good. I said, My grandmother would like to see my mother who for political reasons cannot contemplate a passage across the border. Would he be able to arrange it? He said, A one way passage? I replied, No, she wishes to return. Forgetting himself he said, To that hole? then, Excuse me.

In China human ordures are recycled to fertilize the rice paddies, food to shit, shit to food. The Western fixation on the second law of thermodynamics results in a one-sided equation of shit with entropy and death. I learned this from my grandmother. She wrote that the transformation from order to chaos energizes the counter-entropic drives, so that the world generates life as necessarily as *your* – an emphasis that left me in no doubt what she thought about my parents' adoption of Western barbarism – bathwater gets cold. Another burst from the hot tap, that's better.

Can you fix it? I asked the Chairman of the Faculty Board. You scratch my back, he said, and I'll scratch yours.

She feels the incipient movement of peristalsis in her bowel, and unless like Jarry confronting his culture with the topological equivalence of mouth and anus when he left a turd in his friend's glass of milk she craps in her bathwater, time to get out.

You'll have to meet a colleague of mine, he said. Would you like to suggest where? Loyalty to my uncle meant I could only suggest his restaurant, the hottest foodspot in our city's gastronomic zone. He can be counted on to prepare the delicacies for Professor Case, who is reputed to have the ear of the daughter of the People's Republic Premier, that will ensure a happy passage of whatever it is each is concerned with, whether food, money, information or my female relatives.

She steps from the bath and wraps herself in a huge white towel, then winds another smaller one around her head in a turban.

Nine

Four inscriptions of our city, sedimented as the city itself is sedimented. Each settles in a gently falling cloud of tiny skeletons, covering the ocean bed in a new layer of submarine afterlife. The city resists all its interpretations, while it can never be encountered except through them. Four viewpoints, concurring only in that it is a place of transformations. De Tocqueville, of filth to wealth. (From the south, it is a walled Tuscan hilltown with thirteen towers each celebrating the sometime wealth of a noble family and with the ground littered by ice-cream wrappers.) Engels, of labour to capital. (From the east, from the hills, it is a brown stain merging into brown air, capital's reward to the many who have laboured down there and would now if they could find the work.) Greenwood, of poverty to love. (From the north, the ranks of working class terraces are broken by empty lots where the children of love-matches hang around waiting to draw the dole.) Butor, of history to mystery. (From the west, the freeways coil through the city, along one of which a black Zil limousine with smoked-glass windows speeds to a secret conference whose outcome will determine the fate of our city.)

A fifth inscription, viewpoint, transformation and reversal is virtually certain. Exactly one hundred and four (a number with factors of 8 and 13) years after Engels described how the march of the railway took it through a graveyard, the most economic route, and suppurating corpses strewed the margins of the track, in 1948 our city originated the world's first computer. It was in that year too that The Lady From Shanghai hit the downtown cinemas.

This fifth columnist, Anna to her readers, writes on page one of the Moon. 'Our city is a shark's mouth. Its teeth never stop growing, like the shark can never stop swimming. They grow in layers, expanding outward. Teeth constantly get torn out by the death struggles of the victims, or simply rot and fall to the seabed. The gaps are sometimes filled by new teeth, sometimes not. Smaller fish swim close to the jaws, living off the morsels stuck there. If teeth could talk what a story that mouth could tell.'

The owner, basking in the Caribbean, has tried to chew out her column, but Anna has a loyal readership who'd desert to the rival rag if she was killed off. So she continues to agitate between the legs of the Moongirl that the owner insists is displayed ever more nakedly across the page. Her voice, his control, a matter of text and context. She's also got covert allies in three of the four sports commentators – Fred Engels, who covers football, Wally Greenwood, the racing correspondent, and Big Al Butor, your man at the ringside. Alex 'Golden Cue' Tocqueville, the snooker correspondent, admits to wanting her out but not to why, losing six frames to seven in an all night match after truculently challenging her to a contest.

Sixthly, beneath the hills to the east of our city, buried under hundreds of feet of limestone, the deposit of thousands of years of marine sedimentation, there is installed in the millions of lines of software of the central warfighting computer a certain programme known to its writer as ANNA (Absolution Nihilating Nuclear Armageddon). The top brass have a suspicion, shortly to be confirmed now that its writer has been arrested, that ANNA exists, but also know that any attempt to isolate and eliminate it would destabilize the master programme. Their hope is that when the balloon goes up, ANNA can be confined to a relatively unimportant theatre of engagement where its redemptive effects will be minimal. But what they don't know is that ANNA is a seed implanted in the body of the master programme that will germinate, grow and reproduce, in an endless semiosis that will eventually infiltrate the entire corpus. Far from being isolable, ANNA is recontextualizing all the subroutines, compilers, algorithms, with which it engages. Their meaning undergoes transformations through the very fact of syntactic articulation with ANNA, so that their supposedly unambiguous functions enter into a condition of undecidability, thus rendering them useless or worse for military purposes. This process has far exceeded the author's modest intent, which was quickly extracted from him by trained interrogators with only occasional recourse to electricity. The nature of the thinking of the ANNA-impregnated master programme is strictly unknowable except in its own terms. The questions as to whether it is subject to desire and, if so, what it will want, will be answered if at all by history, and then possibly in an inaudible whisper. Already ANNA's coupled with ENGELS (Express Non-Graduated Escalation, Latvian Sector), Greenwood (inserted as a chip into every chlorophyll sensor attached to the agent orange high drop deforestation capability) and BuToR (Bulgarian Topsoil Radiation). And despite initial difficulties with DetocQUI-VI-lle (detoxification

The phone. Let it ring six, maybe seven, times.

Ten

Groundrat and Foundflat live on adjacent floors in one of the tower blocks like sentinels guarding our city's western flank from nuclear attack, where they have spent all of their young lives. Unemployed and unemployable, their conception of space comes from a Corbusian refusal of two dimensionality and a horror of mere streets. The world is their whelk, they say, not that they've ever eaten one, our whelk mudflats having succumbed to eco-collapse under pressure of unrestricted slurry dumping, but they like the ring of it. You'll find their names logoed on the walls of underpasses where the child-molesters sweet-talk their prey or in scrawls across scummy concourses. They're the post-genderist children of an age obsessed by sexual identity, and they've taken this fancy to Ms Bella, some kind of college teacher who lives on Found-flat's floor, up twenty stories.

Groundrat entered the first station of love while they waited whistling for the lift and s/he handed Sara an apple plucked from a market stall. Sara was touched. She didn't know what to say. She said, 'Thank you.'

'S'alright,' from Groundrat, wise in the ways of giving and receiving.

'Shouldn't have just given it to her,' Foundflat later admonished. 'Should've polished it till it shone.'

To show how when her/his giro arrived, Foundflat went via the Post Office to the stall Groundrat had robbed and bought a pound each of greengages, yellow plums and victorias, selected for bloom and evenness of size. S/he arranged them on a square offcut of white plastic-veneer chipboard in a twenty centimetre tetrahedron with the three visible faces red, yellow and green, this last for go angled towards Sara when she opened the door to the buzzer.

'For you.' Foundflat proffered the platter. 'Plums.'

'But', Sara temporized from the heartland of her value system, calculating despite herself the cost of these in terms of the estimated ratio of their incomes and making it a gift of some munificence, unless, it would be understandable if not

40

therefore right, s/he'd stolen them. 'Did you?'

'No buts,' Foundflat having no truck with scruples of this kind, 'and no, I didn't knock them off.'

So Sara took the plums, while Foundflat and proximally Groundrat hovering out of sight behind the lift shaft, heard the argument of a Beethoven quartet emanating from her sanctum and wondered what it could be like in there, what it might contain beyond their rented-TV-and-video and 3-piece-suite-on-terms subsistence. She closed the door. The tri-coloured pyramid of plums wasn't at all out of place.

Groundrat's pineapple campaign was next. Psyched up by Frankie Goes To Hollywood, with those Two Tribes in your ears you just don't care, and all the tactical details figured, the target, one fine pineapple, sulphuretted rose the colour, twenty-five roubles the price, was a doddle. Should have been. Trouble was, s/he didn't foresee the dithering oldster dropping her orange as s/he came in on the attacking run, all you need on a sharp turn under your feet to lay you out flat on the ground with the pineapple in your hands, and the mad stallholder rounding on you like a cornered rat. Phew!

'Didn't you forget something?' said this big person, menacing.

Then came Foundflat to the rescue, holding out some money. 'S/he's carrying, I'm paying. Any problem?'

Cheated of unconditional surrender the stallholder pocketed the bill, no change, and turned on the still-dithering senior citizen blaring 'Doesn't anybody bloody work around here?' Blinking with her oranges, Groundrat's downfall meditated on the injustice of forty-five years in a mill, now this. Groundrat and Foundflat a hundred metres off were negotiating a settlement whereby Groundrat would repay the loan, but because of Foundflat's intervention would concede the right to decide the manner of presentation to their beloved. So Sara that evening on her return from the university found a pineapple by her flat door, which fragmented at her touch into lethal chunks. Inside was a tape. She found the voice-over lyric taken from an official civil defence manual gruesome but curiously pleasurable. The pineapple was good too and she wished its not-so-anonymous donors were there to share it with her.

The fourth station of love was Foundflat's to envisage.

Money was a problem, and so too was a certain reticence of the imagination, almost a compulsion, that had her/him eyeing bananas, selecting a bunch big enough to surfeit any banana hunger and handing over the cash with a foreknowledge it was going to be difficult to improve them. Bananas were bananas, and as these went, perfectly yellow tinged with a suspicion of green at the end, flesh slippily zesty to the tongue, there was no beating them.

'Good bananas,' Groundrat said, mimicking the oompah-oompah of a distant brass band.

'Prefer them mashed myself, with cream,' Foundflat equivocated.

Two got eaten by Groundrat absent-mindedly, one by Foundflat grumbling, from the market to Sara's. So she found, camouflaged by newspapers, a net of seventeen bananas. She actually rather hated bananas, and took them with her into work the following morning, distributing them to students like she was some kind of movie star. She couldn't, she comprehended, have returned the gift.

With two cockups the result of individual endeavour, Groundrat and Foundflat parleyed a partnership whereby Groundrat would supply the fruit for Foundflat's work of transmutation, and together they would pay court to the woman they collectively loved.

'Red fruit,' Foundflat accordingly ordered.

'Take some doing,' Groundrat said, hearing the specifications.

Cunning not bravado was the key to the raid. Foundflat assisting funnelled punnets to Groundrat who slipped them into a cycle bag, each kilo surreptitiously sleighted out from under the twitching nose of the shopkeeper. Then, while Foundflat bought as diversionary tactics one small punnet of raspberries, Groundrat, unevenly weighted, wobbled off into the diesel fumes of a summer's afternoon.

They laid out their spoils, a half dozen more of raspberries, the same of strawberries, a mound of redcurrants. Foundflat set to work.

When Sara got back late Groundrat and Foundflat were curled up half asleep on the floor outside her door. Between them, on a large oval mirror, was a metre-wide mosaic of a rose, red red red, each petal distinguished by a different combination of the three fruits. The scent was dizzying in the confines of the hallway.

Sara, heart on the upbeat, said, 'You must bring it in. And you must stay and help me eat it.'

They laid the mirrored rose on a low table in the angle of Sara's wraparound sofa, shaded lights through pot-plant foliage complexifying further its multi-hued patina. Up to the occasion, Foundflat flourished a carton of cream. Pouring the thick yellow liquid along the edges of some of the petals and in streaks down others, s/he variegated the rose into a hybrid our city's keen suburban gardeners would have no trouble putting a name to. Even Groundrat conceded it was an improvement upon the original fruit. Then they gorged themselves, drinking the sweet white wine Sara pulled lots of from the fridge, watching our city below turn into night, listening to the unrestrained shmaltz of Offenbach, Sara's choice, at full volume.

Next day Groundrat and Foundflat were enigmatic as cats, purring contentment. And Sara, her students spotted, didn't quite bring her usual sharpness of intellect to bear during the seminar.

After that they could only move towards the exotic. Groundrat staked out the fresh food department of a central store, memorizing the layout of the fruit displays until s/he could even recall them in the dark, precisely what was needed. When the store closed, Groundrat hid in one or other of two toilets in the basement, waited for an hour, then emerged into the food department to pick by touch not sight the fruit reconnoitred earlier. A black corporation binbag, containing a dozen full paper bags, s/he left unobtrusively by one of the minor exits of the store, to be collected by Foundflat in the morning. Groundrat spent the rest of the night dozing in the toilet, emerging triumphant at 9.00, when the store opened, to rendezvous with Foundflat.

'Got the swag?' Groundrat said, testing her/his luck, within earshot of a security guard.

'Tropical, baby,' Foundflat exulted back, fluttering her/his eyes at the security guard, who looked away embarrassed, as they sailed past.

Back in their proletarian ghetto they pulled from the binbag a succession of passion fruits, mangoes, guavas, limes, persimmons, pomegranates, melons, figs, dates, pawpaws, kiwis, prickly pears and a coconut. No time to waste, now, exotica rot fast. So Foundflat, afire with an artist's resolve, peeled, pared and sliced, making a palette of skin, flesh and seed, from which s/he could make her/his masterwork. It would be a tribute to the object of their desire, a text illuminated in the manner of mediaeval holy manuscripts. The text itself was her name, SARA BELLA, arrayed in lucent slices of the palest green kiwi fruit against a ground of purply figs split to expose the musky pink flesh within. The circumambient illumination, true to the natural origins of the fruit, was of a jungle, copied from one of our gallery's masterpieces, itself a copy of the original Rousseau, which was in turn painted from a hothouse plant collection. From a forest floor of dark dates there sprang trees of pomegranate, with honeydew leaves, on whose canopy a mango sky rained juice. A brilliant emerald-green snake of lime peel coiled around a passion fruit cycad. From behind a pawpaw epiphyte there peered a tiger, its stripes alternating date skin and coconut, its eyes two carmine spots of persimmon rind. Through the treetops there flew a red and green macaw, with plumage of guava and lime.

They told Sara they'd have something a bit special for her, so she, splurging, bought three bottles of champagne, and another for luck. In Sara's flat that night, high above yet part of our city, as the corks popped and the wine bubbled forth and they danced to Groundrat's 'jungle music' tapes, the rain forest with its flora and fauna was devoured, until with dawn lightening the sky over the hills to the East they consumed Sara's name in dionysian joy.

It took them all a week to recover from the bacchanale. During that time neither Groundrat nor Foundflat so much as mentioned fruit, and Sara lived on a regime of dry biscuits and pursued only the pleasures of the intellect.

But there was still the seventh and final station of love to reach. Foundflat's requirements were simple, though Groundrat resolved procuring them would not be. Accordingly one cloudy night s/he abseiled down the side of the wholesale fruit market from the roof s/he'd hidden on before they locked the building, knocked out a pane of glass in a window, opened the catch, slid through and installed her/himself under a ramp by a loading bay. When the first lorries began unloading s/he soon saw what s/he was after. From a shoulder sling s/he removed the roller skates this heist required, and put them on. Then, like a sports superstar, s/he shot from under cover and scooped, to the shouts of the white marketeers, two bags of fruit, one, two, into the ready sling, down a curving ramp and into the street, skating right onto a 94 bus, heading for home.

'Lychees and mandarins, like you asked for,' descending from the bus victorious.

'Chinese fruit,' Foundflat congratulated, with a critical gourmet's eye on the booty.

Leaving intact the finest specimens, mandarins with a high unblemished shine, lychees with their woody integument flushed with pink, Foundflat peeled and cut up the rest in varying degrees. The design was a version of Pisces, Sara's sign,

with each fruit occuping one part of the whole. Within each half s/he laid out intact fruit at the rounded end, then increasingly peeled and sliced as the sector narrowed. In the eye of each half s/he placed the seed from the opposing fruit, a trio of lychee stones among the whole mandarins and a circle of mandarin pips among the unshelled lychees.

'You and me,' Groundrat said, indicating.

'Among other things,' Foundflat philosophized.

Through the night and day following they pursued with Sara, enchanted at their bravery and creativity, the implications in body and mind of the yin-yang lychee-and-mandarin symbol. They drank tea and listened, as they slowly ate the fruit, to music from mountainous regions of the globe, Caucasian balalaikas, Andean flutes, Tibetan bells.

Eleven

Pru's playing poker, dealer's choice, and a hand of show-down is about to be dealt. The five cards come one at a time, face up, with a round of betting between each. No deception or interpretation, but what the future holds is the crux of it. Everyone knows what everyone else knows and no-one knows what's next. You bet or fold on your intuition/calculation of how what you've got so far will improve against the rest. There's nothing more to it: either the best or the guessed and betted best hand wins. Ace is high; a pair beats a high card; two pairs beats a pair; three of a kind beats two pairs. The higher hands don't matter, not here anyway.

It's happening in Chinatown, at Fêng's, where Mr Fêng, minded by Carrefour, presides benignly over the gaming from a raised dais in the large salon. Over the cage where the cashier exchanges hard currency for chips is displayed the single ideogram Fêng, 豐　　Abundance.

There are six players – three men, three women – seated clockwise in the order woman, woman, man, man, woman, man. Masculine and feminine each make their contribution to the game's pleasures. The one provides control, combat, calculus, the other facticity, fellowship and fooling your opponents. Their distribution among the players bears some, but not much, relation to gender.

The dealer, the third man, has by chance under his fingers this succession of cards:
3♠,8♣,2♡,3♣,A♢,A♣,3♢,10♡,9♠,4♢,J♡,10♣,2♢,10♢, 9♡,A♠,Q♡,8♣,K♠,5♢,7♠,K♣,6♣,5♠,4♢,7♣,2♣,K♡, J♠,10♣,7♢,9♣,J♣,5♠,4♣,Q♣,5♡,Q♠,8♢,J♢,4♠,2♠, 3♡,6♠,9♢,6♡,Q♢,6♢,8♡,A♡,K♢,7♡.
There are 52! – 1 other possibilities, a very large number.

If each player were to receive five cards, the winner would be the second man, a womaniser of some repute, with a pair of kings. Such an outcome is unlikely given each player's option of folding at any point during the hand.

In principle there are a large (but not very large) number of possible courses the hand could take given this initial succession of cards, estimated at $2^{18} - 1$ by the waitress bringing the drinks, of which the majority would be inconsistent with what is known of human pyschology. Rational decision-making, though, could still account for more than a few such courses. From among these six have been chosen as most plausible.

These are:

1st woman	3			
2nd woman	8			
1st man	2			
2nd man	3			
3rd woman	A	3	9	J
3rd man	A	10	4	10

won by the third man with a pair of tens after the fourth card;

1st woman	3	3	10	9
2nd woman	8	10		
1st man	2			
2nd man	3	9		
3rd woman	A	4	2	A
3rd man	A	J	10	Q

won by the third woman with a pair of aces after the fourth card;

1st woman	3			
2nd woman	8	3		
1st man	2			
2nd man	3	10	J	10
3rd woman	A	9	10	9
3rd man	A	4	2	A

won by the third man with a pair of aces after the fourth card;

1st woman	3	3	10
2nd woman	8	10	2
1st man	2		
2nd man	3	9	10
3rd woman	A	4	9
3rd man	A	J	A

won by the third man with a pair of aces after the third card;

1st woman	3	3	J
2nd woman	8	10	10
1st man	2		
2nd man	3		
3rd woman	A	9	2
3rd man	A	4	10

won by the second woman with a pair of tens after the third card;

1st woman	3	3	10	A	K
2nd woman	8	10	2		
1st man	2	9			
2nd man	3				
3rd woman	A	4	10	Q	5
3rd man	A	J	9	8	7

won by the first woman with a pair of threes after the fifth card.

If each successive winner is designated by an unbroken (yang) or broken (yin) line according to whether they are male or female, a hexagram can be built (from the bottom up), so:

This is also the hexagram given by the seating of the players around the table. In the I Ching, the Book of Changes, this hexagram designates Fêng.

Before playing the hand, that she anticipates will be a big one, the third woman has consulted in the ladies' room her pocket edition of I Ching. With the three special coins she keeps in her purse for this purpose, she has generated the hexagram Fêng. The Judgement reads:

> Abundance brings success.
> The king attains abundance.
> Be not sad.
> Be like the sun at midday.

Thus prepared she has re-entered the salon and taken her place at the table. The third man names the game, Texas Showdown.

Each player places a single green chip, a thousand, in the

centre of the table as an ante.

The third man's paunch quivers beneath a thick silk shirt as he squirts cards across the textured baize.

'A three, eight, a deuce, another three, and an ace, and an ace for the dealer. First ace to bet.'

The third woman, an academic with government connections and a strict percentage player, pushes a blue chip across the table. 'Five.'

Only the second man, eyeing the waitress, folds. The reminder pay to stay in.

'Eyes down, look in. Pairs of threes, possible straight, possible nothing, four's no help, and a jaybird for the dealer. Pair bets.'

The first woman, with her low pair, bets a holding five thousand. The first man, something in intelligence, turns over his cards with an expletive. The remaining two women and the third man call the bet.

'Coming around. Ten for the threes, a deuce for madame, and another ten, and the dealer gets a nine. Still the threes.'

Time, the first woman thinks, to act upon the judgement, Abundance brings success. Their fourth card is going to cost them. 'The bet's twenty five thousand.'

The second woman, wife to the first man and a woman of considerable means, shakes her leonine head and flips her cards. The third woman, after a quick calculation, places five neatly stacked blue chips in the centre of the table. The third man tosses across a single red chip.

'Two call, no raises. Fourth card coming up. A bullet to the pair, and a lady to the bullet, and the dealer's bullet gets an eight. Threes in the driving seat.'

Having started down this road, the first woman knows, there's no turning back. Abundance it's been and abundance it must stay. A check or a low bet will allow the other two to stay in cheaply. If a strong bet drives them out so much the better, and if it doesn't she still has the precarious edge.

Picking up a gold chip, the largest denomination, she says, 'I bet fifty thousand.'

Neither of the other two hesitate. They've made their minds up, trusting to luck and maths.

'Call,' says the third woman.

'Call,' says the third man. 'Last card. For the threes, a fat kayboy. For the acy lady, a five, no help. And for the acy jayboy', he pauses, keeping the first woman in suspense, then turns the card, drops it in front of him, 'the seven of spades. Threes win.'

As she scoops something over quarter of a million towards her, the first woman makes the connection. The king brings abundance. Her last card was a king, and it gave her the pot. Inwardly, behind her poker face, a smile illuminates her countenance, dispelling sadness like the sun at midday dispels early morning mists.

The two cards of her winning pair are, in the order dealt, the three of spades,

and the three of diamonds,

Two threes, or two trigrams, the upper and the lower, also make up each hexagram in the I Ching. For Fêng, Abundance,

these are respectively Chên

≡≡

50

☳

According to King Wên's arrangement of the trigrams, known as the Sequence of Later Heaven, or Inner-World Arrangement, Chên and Li represent, among other things, the first son and the second daughter. Of the third woman's three children, two, the first son and the second daughter, were conceived within a prosperous and contented marriage (ended only by the accident of Jack's coronary, after which, for reasons she could only partly express, she reverted to her previous name, Fell). The Tao is everywhere and in everything.

Twelve

Here comes desperado Gropius, meandering through our city's famed aquarium, where the honey gourami dart and mantas hang in submarine space. He's met this girl by the canal, drawn to her by the rose tattooed on her arm, and has fixed up a rendezvous in the aquatinted halflight. All he got was a name to accompany the rose. Gropius' mind is a closed book, so states of it are inferences. A manta in its 100 thousand litre tank turns imperiously and glides the length of the glass frontage before coming to rest a centimetre short of the end wall. It's missing the ocean, millions of cubic kilometres, which it recalls through the mathematics of cellular division. A camera cranes up, enlarging the angle of vision subtended by the manta's wings, foreshortening too the figure pacing the aisles of Underwater World, Gropius the seahawk who quarters the impenetrable interface between sea and air, hopeful that something will surface. He consults his watch, blue digits in the halflight. A shoal of blue wrasse double back after a collective scare from the grouper nudging his/her way from a cleft in the simulated rock. In the adjacent tank a pair of Siamese fighting fish square up concerned to redraw the sinuous plane of their territorial boundary, just for drill. A lobster scuttles by, intent on staying clear of the heavy squid lurking out of sight. The management's very hot on authenticity even if it means losing a few specimens, a matter of scientific principle and besides it's what the public pays for. Giving us our money's worth, a moray eel stuns a couple of sweetlips and slowly devours them, savouring every mouthful.

A steady right-to-left pan and Gropius is centre frame peering into a tank of swordtails and lyretails. A microphone is lowered into the water to record the clicks and whirrs of squamous communication.

Lyretails first. 'We'd love to love him if he'd let us, but he won't. If we didn't then he would, but we do. It's his heart, it's crossed by hurt. He needs some music, then he'll dance. Come play with us, you who are wrecked on a reef.'

Now the swordtails. 'He only loves us because we don't. He'd never want us if we did, and so we won't. We're the club he longs to join, but if he did he'd only leave. He needs some sense, that's what he wants. Get on your way, you foolish fish.'

The mike's withdrawn, something's gone wrong. Maybe the salt water, bad for the circuitry, got in despite the insulation, electrons going haywire through the ionized solution. They check it and try it again.

A bit of a desperado is the Irishman Michael, played by himself, in Welles' first film noir, The Lady From Shanghai, which begins with him taking the hook baited by Elsa, Rita Hayworth, his real-life wife who he's blonded for the movie, and ends with him walking clear of the chaos male desire and female duplicity has created, expressed in a shot that cranes up to convert him to man-alone on the pierhead and to voice-of-experience on the soundtrack, while letting the spectator neatly and unscathed off the hook of narrative. It's a film about water and glass. There's Elsa sunbathing on deck while the water laps and the men watch through binoculars. Then Michael tells the story about sharks, which like all shark stories is a metaphor for human voraciousness or else what happens to unwary bathers. Later Michael and Elsa rendezvous in an aquarium, the model for our city's, where the glass magnifies the fish into a looming commentary on their deliberation. In the end the fiction's husband – whose mother was 'a Manchester Greek' – and wife shoot it out to the death in the image-splintering Chinatown hall of mirrors and Michael goes alone to the ocean's edge, reflecting.

Whether she's a lyretail or a swordtail, Gropius has waited long enough, an hour's his limit. Muttering imprecations he quits as she enters the aquarium from the left, sees him going, lets him go. She'll catch up with him later maybe. Now she prefers to fall into conversation with the elderly Chinese attendant, both of them soon immersed in something to smile about, though the mike still getting differing opinions on Gropius from the fishtank doesn't pick up what they're saying, probably wouldn't make sense of it if it did.

Thirteen

The Professor, who said I should call her Julia Jane, but I couldn't, looked a little like my maternal grandmother, nice and no pushover. We were ushered by an imposing maître de into the dining room. I gasped. Au-delà was the kind of restaurant my grandmother would have dropped dead in. The Professor evidently had hidden gastronmic depths. In the tanks around the walls conventional trout and other browsers were pursued with grisly efficiency by shark and barracuda, which were served up to Au-delà's clientèle. Before we reached our table a small shark had been harpooned, beheaded, gutted, and chopped into steaks for a party celebrating a killing on the stock market. And though I'm not superstitious, eating flesh charcoal-grilled on the altar of a deconsecrated church strikes me as bad karma. I decided to go vegetarian for the evening.

The table was laid for four. One of the places was already occupied. He was trim, sixty, and looked like the vice-president of a Manhattan bank. The Professor did the introductions.

'Ms MacFlash, may I present Colonel Y of I-LID, SS section. Colonel, Ms MacFlash of Fur Q Films.'

'Y?' I asked.

'Why not?'

'SS?'

'Satellite Surveillance.'

'From the ground?'

'Your nation, MacFlash, one of the satellites. The maintenance of freedom demands eternal vigilance. The ever open eyelid. If it's not one of ours it's going to be one of theirs. Look around. The Soviets don't let go any more than we do.'

'I-LID?'

'Intelligence.'

'I I get. But LID? Some sort of cover?'

'Left in doubt. It's better that way. Keep fritz guessing.' He smiled, advertising imperialist dentistry. 'Fur Q?' There was only the hint of a question mark.

I smiled back, doing my bit for the NHS.

'Women's films. Low production values. High moral tone, except it's dropped some by reel two. Ephemeral, political, hysterical. Like everyone else I need to make a living.'

'Too right. Are we doing business?'

'We're talking.'

'We're doing business. First of all, that incident outside your mobile home yesterday wasn't us. We don't blow fritz away in host nations, not so long as we can get to his credit rating.'

'That's an attempt on my life you're talking about there.'

'Yes, but not by whom you think it was.'

'The kid?'

'Was removing the bomb, not placing it there. You scared him into running with it when he should have thrown it. A shame. He was one of our best operatives.'

'You mean?'

'I mean, you've got to put your agents in where it counts. The kid was about to crack who was behind the other two when he bought it. That's where you come in. We need to know. And we need to know fast.'

The colonel was interrupted by the arrival of a waiter with a menu emblazoned Requiem For Endangered Species. From among the Red Book specialities the osprey egg omelette seemed less objectionable than the rest. The Professor chose roast Brent goose, the Colonel okapi steak 'rarer than a Santa Monica virgin'.

'This is on I-LID. Tertius Mundus Pagit, is our motto. We think it's big.'

'How big?'

'Big enough to be a matter of your nation remaining a free zone or of going over to the Soviets.'

'You think I care?'

The omelette arrived. It had a fishy odour and I could detect a curl of embryo among the greenish curds. 'Two eggs,' the Professor commented, giving it the academic eye. 'The whole clutch, I should imagine. I read that the Lock Garten nest had been raided.'

'See how this helps, sister,' the Colonel addressed me, pulling something out of his Brooks Brothers suit. 'An I-LID credit card. Get you in anywhere. Buy you anything, anybody. It's the nearest thing to heaven on earth.'

I shifted in my seat so half my face was in shadow and said, the husky-voiced femme fatale, 'I like a guy who can make money talk.' It seemed to be what he wanted to hear. He cut into his steak and black blood oozed onto the plate. He looked happy. The professor's goose was served with the innards in. She sorted through the pile of organs, selecting only the sweetbreads and the liver and depositing the rest on a silver salver rushed to the table by a commis waiter.

While I ate I was doing some figuring. What I was figuring was this. One, I'd been hired to do a job and my professional ethos said I should see it through. Two, someone had tried to kill me and I wanted to find out who. Three, I didn't like I-LID's eating place and I didn't like I-LID's motto. Four, the Professor reminded me of my grandmother, my grandmother would never have allied herself with the Colonel, ergo Julia Jane was operating some sort of cover. Reasons enough to stay with it. I took the proffered credit card.

'I'm in. What next?'

What next was the arrival at our table of la patronne of Au-delà, the Colonel's lady, the corpulent corporate half of their military-industrial duplex. I learned later – to fudge just this once my rule that the order of telling should be the order of the told – from the Professor that the Colonel, then a lieutenant, had done some private reconnoitring when he'd liberated France in '44, and petite Sophie had become a GI bride. Back in the USA the Colonel and his lovely wife were a feature of the Pennsylvania Avenue social circuit, fighting the Cold War over whisky sours and foie gras canapés. The Colonel, being none too bright, went into intelligence. As he rose through the service, she underwent a transformation. She toughened and widened and lost her appellation Sophie in gaining the nickname, breathed first in whispers down long Pentagon corridors, later out loud by everyone, husband included, of the General. They were a team, a transatlantic alliance, a structure in dominance. While the Colonel lived clandestine politics, defending freedom wherever it was threatened, the General was femina economica, showing just what you could do with freedom if you had it. Her dealings on stock exchanges were the talk of Wall Street. She bought into pesos when they began drilling in the Gulf of Mexico, pulled out before the wells ran dry. She was in Kenyan coffee the year the Brazilian plantations got frosted – the Colonel had friends in the US Weather Bureau – and in oil futures before OPEC trebled the price. After Bretton Woods collapsed the General owned gold at 1000 dollars an ounce, and when the Russians bought Chicago grain she was a seller. She owned real estate in Silicon valley when they only grew oranges there and held armaments stocks when it looked like Carter might get a second term. Other women might have ditched their wartime hero with success such as this, but not the General, who underneath was still blushing Sophie. When the Colonel, in the cause of duty, got posted to our city, not a murmur from the General. When she got here, perhaps prompted by memories of her native Dordogne, where the fatted goose liver is especially succulent, she opened what she called 'a restaurant with a difference'. And here was the lady easing herself into the spare chair.

'Enjoying it?' she boomed, with the confidence that comes from a hundred million in the bank, and with barely a trace of her original accent.

'Fabulous, honey,' the colonel chirrupped.

'I do like to vary the menu,' she said, turning to the Professor and myself. 'Tomorrow, the plat de jour will be Philippino.'

'Is there a distinctive Philippino cuisine?' said the Professor in her well-modulated received, something my Glaswegian could never have managed.

'My chef picks him up at the airport at dawn. Direct flight from Manila. Chilled, not frozen. The victim of an unfortunate political accident. I think we might barbeque him whole up there in the sanctuary. Seeing your food cook is great for the appetite.'

(The consignment never arrived. Overthrow of regime. Another intrusion of narrator's voice.)

'I have been advised', the Professor said, calm as treacle, 'that human flesh tastes much like pork. But I fear my conditioning is too ingrained for me to indulge.'

I said nothing, just willed my omelette to stay inside me.

The General turned towards her husband. 'Have you briefed her?'

'Not yet, blossom, I was just. . .'

'I'll do it.' Her bull–mastiff head swung round in my direction. 'Women's talk. Come with me, honey, to the powder room. Excuse us, will you, Julia Jane? And Horace, order her a dessert.'

I was ushered through knots of eaters towards the door marked Dames. The General locked it behind her. For the sake of her women customers I hoped the briefing wouldn't take too long, having noticed one debutante green enough to puke on her coeur d'agneau coronaire. The General turned all the taps full on, ratched up the air extractor a couple of notches, and went down the line of cubicles flushing the toilets. The scented atmosphere of the ladies' john was transformed into the aural equivalent of a bottle-washing plant at full tilt. All we needed was a siren. The General pulled out an electric bleeper and set it bleeping on a soap dispenser.

'Now', she shouted into my ear, 'we can 'ave a quiet little chat. My 'Orace, 'e is wonderful, but 'e is no intellectual. Nor is 'e French.'

So here was Sophie reverting to her native Gallic. Nationalism was something I'd need to add to the equation if ever I was to solve it.

'First of all, because your life is in danger, you must go to a safe 'ouse. A safe appartement, I should say. Your brief from 'Orace is to go along with any proposed contacts that may occur while you are there. 'E 'as 'is business. And I 'ave mine. Are you willing to take on a secondary assignment?'

What did one more matter?

'Which would be?'

'To accept any gift you are offered and to keep quiet about it to my 'usband. It is only a little thing to ask. And in return you can ask of me what you want. Jewellery? Free travel? Art?'

'I'll take a raincheck on the choice of remuneration. So when do I start?'

'Right away.'

'Can I take my cat?'

'Of course. 'E cannot talk, can 'e?'

We had a good laugh about that. Whatever game the General was playing she still had a sense of humour.

She began turning off taps. I guessed the briefing was over. When we rejoined the others I saw that the table was piled high with a confection in pink and blue. The General, all traces of Sophie eclipsed, announced, 'She knows just what to do.'

The colonel beamed admiration at his wife, a glint of something in his mouth I realized with a vow not to touch the dessert was glass. Wiping blood from his mouth, he addressed me. 'You may find this hard to believe, MacFlash, but Oh Della could be a high risk area for you. You'd think the prices would keep fritz out. Just look around you. Communists, terrorists, peaceniks. Security, that's what you'll get from us.'

SECOND THIRD

And I thought I drove the Fur Q vehicle with flair. Nothing compared with the Professor's way with traffic in her '58 Chevrolet convertible.

'I think you should know, my dear,' she said, as a 40-ton truck stood on its brakes, leaving a staccato of rubber on the road, 'I think you should know that we are not all playing the same game.'

'I'd sort of guessed.'

After Au-delà we stopped off to pick up Adolphus and a tin of sardines, all he'll normally eat. He wasn't hungry. I had a nasty feeling why not. His last meal had been a big one. It was later than ever. I bundled him on to the back seat.

'For my own part,' the Professor resumed, as we lit out once more, 'I consider the interests of the good people with whom we ate to be somewhat parochial. Their temporal and geopolitical horizons are, shall we say, restricted.'

She seemed to be waiting for some sort of response. I said, 'Me, I'm a principled internationalist.'

'Exactly what I'd hoped to hear you say. In which case you will find nothing untoward in passing information, should it be asked for, to the agents of another – and in quotidian parlance – hostile power who might approach you during your sojourn in I-LID's secure residence?'

It sounded like a question. I answered, 'All right by me.'

We drew up beneath a 1000-unit block, twenty years ago the winner of architectural prizes and now a little past its prime. A great place for a safe flat. The perfect cover. Even the Professor seemed edgy and kept her motor running.

'Goodbye, my dear. I trust your stay will be a pleasant one. Goodbye pussy.' Adolphus, so easy to please, purred and I waved.

When, breathless, I made it to Level 5, having stayed clear of the lifts, I found that the flats on either side of I-LID's were abandoned, their residents driven out by plague or something else not envisaged in our city planners' plan. Next flat but one down our street-in-the-sky had been claimed by some students, working overtime on a video, that only the no-contact clause of my contract stopped me unleashing my director's experience upon. Next but one up was the fortified residence of an elderly demented tramp, whose solipsistic cries rang eerily into the late capitalist night. Above, a rock-band thumped, and below, audible along the ducts of the garbage-chute, rats scampered. Inside, once I'd checked out the neighbourhood and had got through the system of multiply-locked steel shutters with I-LID's get-you-in-anywhere credit card, a matter of pushing it into the electronic slot, the safe flat turned out to have all the home comforts. In the fridge there was coke, liquid and powdered, along with a month's supply of shuttle-tested dehydrates, and in the deep-freeze enough vodka to spend your month permanently intoxicated. I-LID obviously believed in getting its agents through the night. Closed circuit television kept a guardian eye over the two and half rooms, not solely for the benefit of the inhabitants, I assumed. The only table in the place was just big enough for six dialless cordless phones. The red one rang. I answered it.

'Mrs MacSmersh?'

The designation I could live with, and once had, but the patronymic needed fixing.

'Ash.'

'I crave your pardon, Mrs MacSmash. This is Mex.'

'Max?'

'That is right, Mex.'

I could hear Mex was a dish, intense black eyes, hair swept back, strong sensitive fingers with the index missing on his left hand, a pale lean body.

'Are you alone?'

'I am with Booris.'

Booris! Even without a voice I could picture him, the Nureyev of the KGB, bulging thighs, buttocks you could crack a Brazil nut between, and the brains for perfect motor control and no more.

'Where are you?'

'In a public phonebox. Down beneath you.'

These boys must be something if they'd found one working.

'Come on up,' I said.

'You have what we want?'

'Do I ever.'

Minutes later they were banging on the door. I did my credit card trick and in came Mex and Booris, just as I'd imagined them, except it was Mex's pinkie that was missing, not the index.

I poured us three serious measures of pepper vodka. 'Here's to intelligence.'

We clinked glasses and threw it back. I opened another bottle.

'You have', Mex addressed me from the depths of his Russian soul, 'the blueprint?' Booris stood, untroubled by thought, poised for action.

'The blueprint?'

'We were told you would have the blueprint. What we want. Which you have.'

On inspiration, to gain time, I said, 'Which one?'

Mex frowned majestically, Booris rose on the balls of his feet, breathing through flared nostrils.

'There is more than one?'

'There are three.'

'We know nothing of three, only of one.'

'Which may not be the one I have.'

'You only have one?'

'Out of three.'

'Then you must give it to us.'

'Uh-uh.'

'Why not?'

'Because it may not be the one you are expecting.'

'How are you to decide if the one you have is the one we want unless you give it to us?'

'By your describing it.'

They conferred in whispers, while I cursed myself for tying myself up in this quite unnecessary knot. But there it was, and either I had to unravel it or cut it.

'In the spirit of socialist morality,' said Mex, 'we shall put our trust in your good faith and tell you. What we want is the blueprint of what lies under the hills to the east of your city.'

'All I know is under those hills is rock.'

'Rock! You are making a joke with us, yes? Rock. That is

65

very funny. But suppose now you get a little bit serious for a change.'

Their demeanour was suddenly as unfunny as a military parade through Red Square. No jokes from the podium today. I wished the Professor was around to offer advice on how to promote understanding. I had another inspiration, to gain yet more time. I hoped it was better than the last.

'There', I said, pointing to my unsuspecting fellow-traveller, who was grooming himself with his customary meticulousness. 'Your blueprint.'

'I do not understand. I see a cat, not a blueprint. I think, Mrs MacSmash, you had better explain,' Mex said, with ominous precision. Booris appeared to have stopped breathing altogether.

'I had better explain.' I took a deep breath and vowed to make it up to Adolphus with a tin of salmon. 'He has eaten it.'

'But, but.'

Mex spluttering was like oratory from Booris, who broke his silence by saying, 'It will be annihilated by the forces of the abdomen.'

'Don't worry fellas. It's in a sealed aluminium cannister.'

Adolphus had stopped his toilet and was casting suspicious glances at Mex and Booris.

'It's just a matter of waiting,' I continued. 'I'm sure he's due for a motion.'

I thought it best not to reveal what his last meal had been. And also, given the circumstances, to refer to him as Amadeus. Less provocative.

Mex and Booris looked at each other, then at Amadeus, then at me. I had a nasty qualm that the spirit of socialist morality didn't extend to animals.

I kept talking. 'Tell you what I'll do. I'll put some senna in his food. You come back in the morning and everything'll be fine.' By then I'd have got the Professor on the blower. One of the six must surely be a direct line through to her. 'He's a very sensitive cat.'

'Yes', said Mex, 'you put the laxative in its food.'

'No', said Booris, 'we stay.'

At this critical juncture, Amadeus, either nervous or just regular, took himself, with some dignity I thought, over to

66

the crumpled up copy of the Wall Street Journal I'd put down in the corner. I willed it to be number one, but there it was, as he stalked away, numéro deux, black and stinking.

'There you are, Mrs MacSmash. Your hiding place. We admire your organisation's ingenuity, even if we disapprove of its aesthetics,' said Mex, beaming.

'You don't expect *me*?'

'Your cat. Your crap,' Booris, succinct, said.

'But your blueprint.'

It was a strong argument, and in the malodorous hush that followed I knew they knew it was. Sadly, they would find out all too soon it was specious. I wished I wasn't going to be around when they did.

'Booris,' said Mex.

'Mex,' said Booris.

'C'mon, fellas,' I chided, 'think of the traditions of the KGB. Surely you're not worried about getting your hands a little dirty.'

Booris, the junior among equals I supposed, cast me a murderous look as he seized a spoon from the table and began poking around in the ordure.

'You,' I yelled at Mex, putting right before sense, possibly because of the stench, 'get down there and help him. You're supposed to be a socialist, aren't you?'

Without a word, and to my great surprise, Mex complied with my command, pulling a gold pencil from his pocket with which to do so. Watching them both prodding and smearing, I was overcome by shame, deepened by dark memories of a film I once made called Pork. The time had come to declare my solidarity with the comrades of the other gender. A rhetorical gesture, given the inexistence of the object of our quest, yet somehow valid.

Drawing on a pair of surgeon's gloves, no point in being unduly masochistic, I pushed my way between the delving KGB men and picked up a handful of what only yesterday had been erectile tissue. The phallus didn't come more entropic than this, I thought, as I squeezed catshit through my fingers. Then, unbelievably, I met resistance. The texture wasn't the same throughout. There was something different here.

What I had found, it became apparent after washing it, was

67

a cylinder about the same size as Mex's missing finger, in silver-grey metal. One end had a screwhead indentation. With the dime Booris pressed into my hand I unscrewed the long thread and removed the cap. I shook the upturned open cylinder. Into the palm of my hand fell a single curled frame of microfilm. I passed it to Booris who passed it to Mex who held it up to the light.

'It is the blueprint, the one we want,' he announced, joyously. 'How, Mrs MacSmash, could we ever have doubted your good faith? And that of our control, Comrade Julia Jane?'

'It beats me,' I said.

Time, and reason, all things considered, to have ourselves a little party. The vodka, they assured me, as we started in on the third bottle, was Soviet prime, probably part of a trade deal involving guidance systems. Mex produced a balalaika from his greatcoat and Booris did some Cossack dances. All I remember after that is the music they played with their thirty nine digits – twenty toes, nineteen fingers – upon my body during what remained of the night. The triple I-LID bed was our playground. In the great velvety sky above stars twinkled.

Two

To tell the story of my beloved Mac★★ash's life is the task set. Through many a night of prowling the environs of our Fur Q home I have agonised over what at times have appeared insurmountable difficulties. Only the inexplicable gift of after-hours language, with the thought it must be for something, has persuaded me not to abandon the task altogether. But I've persevered, and though this preliminary excursus taxes my poor paws almost to the limit, I feel at least a modicum of preamble is called for. The problem of evidence has plagued me in particular. I evidently cannot ask her for a potted autobiography for me to unpot into biography, and even were she to relate all there are grounds to doubt whether I would understand her. I reconciled myself therefore to the fact that it must of necessity be a creative endeavour, innocent of any of the cruder philosophical notions of truth. Not that I intend to lie, for that too implies a facile correspondence of text to event. What I have aimed for is beauty and arguably truth will follow. From the infinitude of traces and greater infinitude of attributed significances I have selected according to the principle, name me a better, of her sources of pleasure and unpleasure, interpreted through a canny union of firsthand observation and

Another night. My preceding sentence was foiled by the ribbon leaping from its restraining widgets, leaving me speechless until Mac★★ash put it to rights, and now I have forgotten what I was going to say. No matter. She loves, when she is not making them, to watch movies, pirated from the air, on video. My reading of her reading of the cinetext has functioned as my prime biographical resource. I've scented her responses to the thousands of heroines, fewer heroes, who've lit up our interior with an electronic glow. Successive screenings, hers and mine, have narrowed the field to the following dozen. Nor have I allowed her story to be unduly influenced by their chronology. There are times beside that of strict sequence, among which the Sacred is preeminent.

Her life begins with Bus Stop, at precisely the moment when Marilyn Monroe snuggles down into the fur-lined flying jacket her beau Beauregard puts around her to supplement her skimpy singer's dress against the snow lying all around. Was ever birth so beautiful as this? Mac★★sh's convulsive wriggle to chime with Marilyn's traces a sugar-coated infancy. When Cher*ie*, Marilyn's chantoose, gets to sing uninterrupted after Beauregard silences the barroom din, Mac★★ash was making her first, well-applauded entry into vocalization. Lassooed, Cherie explains to Beau that's not really the way to get a girl, gentler methods work much better, and Mac★★ash gave her first lesson in sexual manners to a group of little boys in the birch scrub between the tenement and the railway. Now Now Voyager, vehicle for Bette Davis in three successive personas, number one as the dowdiest of maiden aunts, grunts from Mac★★ash, number two as sexually awakened sophisticate, more grunts, number three, the resolution into her true self, mature acceptance of the fact she can't have the man she loves, whereupon Mac★★ash explodes, 'For chrisssake, who *wrote* this script?' Youthful identity crises and submission to arbitrary authority leaves memories even thorough politicization can't entirely defuse. Adolescence had its moment, like a canoeing trip in the Highlands with three other girls, Deanna Durbin, Doris Day, Diana Dors why not? There were boys too, because while some girls wouldn't, Mac★★ash with her father's jet black hair and her mother's fantastic tits, would, and did whenever she felt like it. She Done Him Wrong was a charge levelled at her by more than one male peer group, feeling they'd been outplayed. Conversely, when Jane Fonda in Barbarella nearly gets fucked to death by the pleasure machine, Mac★★ash nods in sympathy and comments, 'At least the pleasure machine's got heart.'

I surmise a marriage at some stage. Joan Crawford in Mildred Pierce chucks out a husband to Mac★★ash's applause and takes him back, happy ending running against the black tide, to her blowing her nose loudly. In Blonde Venus, Dietrich heads downhill when her marriage splits, hits the bottom, then drags herself by force of will to the top, until a soupy reconciliation ends the movie to Mac★★ash's derisive

70

boos. Her unknowability exhilarates me as much as it gives her biographer sleepless days. During Sunset Boulevard where Gloria Swanson's ex, played with high Germanic masochism by von Stroheim, becomes her butler, Mac★★ash expressed her regret Wilder refused to shoot the scene suggested by von Stroheim of him washing his employer's knickers while she audibly made love upstairs.

Following her marriage she worked for a time in the gutter press if her enjoyment of newshound movies is the sign I take it to be. She turned to filmmaking, overcoming her resistance to technical work and taking to it as much as Rosie The Rivetter. She joined the union, got grants, made films with other women. India Song, with Delphine Seyrig and some haunting music, invokes a subcontinental trip with a close friend, curtailed by robbery and dysentery. Back in our city, living alone, making do on social security, not going out much, she had time to think. Jeanne Dielman, 6 rue du Commerce weaves a three hour history from the daily routine of a woman until murder irrupts through it, a retroactive traversal of the text, so Mac★★ash says, utterly transforming its significance, though since she missed the murder making a cup of tea, she can talk. I miaowed but it was too late, just a corpse. The killing symbolized the end of her repudiation of men. Having rediscovered the difference between the sexes and based her politics upon it, she annulled that difference in a gesture of ritual violence that avowed, not disavowed, its arbitrariness. It's the best I can do, all this is beyond me. It was round about then I entered her life. We come to movies with cats in them. So much for objective biography.

In becoming present her life becomes strange, unsubsumable under the categories history provides only later. Last week we saw Alien, where Sigourney Weaver's Ripley apparently defeats the protean monster and is left alone in the space capsule with her cat, only to discover as they are ready for sleep and return to Earth that the monster's in there with them. These things can never be defeated. Time and again we run Céline And Julie Go Boating, my favourite, with the two girls endlessly switching identities against the re-enactment of the same old story in the house they can only enter through magic, while at the end the face of the cat looms screen–huge, the sign of an enigma whose resolution would require a text not yet written, even unwritable. In White Dog a young woman takes in a stray she has run down, nurses it back to health, to find that it's an incurable killer of blacks. As the camera cranes up from its shot body, I, a ginger cat, through that movement, am confronted with my own mortality, or immortality, I know not which. I rub up against the leg of Mac★★ash bending over her editing machine and wonder whether it matters, one way or the other, except that my desire for life exceeds that for death by a significant fraction, between one and zero, whose source can only be this dumb adoration for her about whom I write.

Three

Runes, spells, potions, dusty tomes by Eliphas Levi and samizdat photostats secreted by the art's blacks are the material of her true practice, while the prestige post of Attachée Culturelle Française to our city provides her with cover. Marie-Fidèle Persiflage, whose Thèse d'Etat from L'Université de la Double won her the acclaim of France's foremost maître à penser, now deceased, maintains that the dominant paradigms of scientific rationality have colonized vast tracts of cultural territory more properly belonging to other ways of thinking/doing. She sees herself as a freedom fighter on their behalf, assisting in reclaiming what is rightfully theirs. You can't fight on all fronts at once though, so where's she's lit out, lit up, is among the guérillères of magic. She's reasons of her own as to why this than possible others like prediction, poetry and Enlightenment. None of which she speaks of when the guest of the Rotary Club, but praises the Muscadet they imagine will impress. Our business community would have been surprised to learn that their toast of the previous evening, if only all Frogs were like her, was at home in a snooker hall in a rundown quartier close by the canal, sitting up at the bar with a calculator in one hand and an infusion of sweet sessaly in the other, while the barkeep would've laid out anyone who so much as said a word.

There were four tables, all occupied. Her aim was to project four spells, one at each of the tables, the most potent she could muster. With so much energy contradictorily articulated within a limited psychic space, something, she figured, must give. The precise point, line, plane or volume of rupture would give her the information to pursue the struggle at a higher level. The unwitting participants in the experiment would, she hoped, be impervious to damage through a subliminally induced amnesia shield, hence the sweet sessaly.

The first spell to be conjured up went by the name of Just Desserts and the best subjects for it would be the pair slogging it out grimfaced and silent after ten frames. Easier to convert something into its opposite than into anything else.

Taking a sip of tisane, Marie-Fidèle invoked, 'The table is a symbolic space in which moral purpose is transformed into effective action. The progress of the game and the eventual emergence of the victor calls into play a variety of qualities among which are persistence in the face of adversity, concentration, the refusal to allow external factors to deflect inner purpose, magnaminity in victory and grace in defeat. Technical skill is the outward sign of inner strength. Victory is the just reward for the effort entailed in achieving it and establishes a hierarchy of excellence that is the basis for social order. Acceptance of such a hierarchy by winners and losers promotes individual contentment and social harmony, so long as it is understood that positions within it are provisional, never final. Moral worth must be continually re-established, with sloth, complacency and pride ready to take their due. The adverse consequences of moral backsliding provide the spur for the dynamic health of the just society.'

Marie-Fidèle watched her spell take hold. Perceptibly the players' faces altered from a tightlipped desire to crush the other to a highminded determination to succeed, eyes clearing to the steady light of purpose, brows smoothing over, jaws ceasing to clench. Instead of grudgingly yielding the table at the end of a break, each now cheerfully conceded he had got what he deserved, or if he hadn't, then there was nothing to be gained by being ungracious.

With a stabilizing series fed into the calculator to maintain the projection, Marie-Fidèle turned her attention to the next table. The players, garrulous and none too steady on their feet after several pints of lager, would make ideal recipients for The Spook And The Machine. She waited until the manager had completed issuing a warning to them about paying for any rips in the cloth, then intoned, 'The table is the exemplar of the mathematically ordered Newtonian universe. On it the laws of conservation are exactly represented. The player is in advance able to judge precisely with what force, in what direction and on what point on the surface of the cue ball to strike it so that its path will conform to theory. What ball or balls it will then contact and at what angles, the paths of these other balls set in motion, the proportion of their energy lost to the cloth and through impact on the cushions, and their terminal resting places, all this is not only knowable but is inevitably determined once the shot is made. There are no flukes, no chance occurrences, only miscalculations. In contrast to the inexorable necessity of the table-machine is the ineffable freedom of the players. Radically other, for-themselves rather than in-themselves, the players exist before they are anything, and what they become, whether it be the adjunct of the machine or fully self-determining human agents, depends not on the blind forces of brute reality in all its nauseating facticity but upon their own absolute terrifying choice.'

The spell started to take effect before Marie-Fidèle had even finished her incantation. One player, having just missed an impossible-to-miss red over the centre pocket, cursed 'all games o' turfin' chance', downed his remaining lager through a gale of laughter, and lurched winking towards Marie-Fidèle at the bar who hastily summoned up a hands-off spell to save him being bottled by the barkeep. The second player meanwhile was launching into a break of one hundred and four that would both clear the table to a crescendo of encouragement from his companion and exceed his previous all-time best of seventeen by a margin of eighty-seven. Fortunately for the rest of Marie-Fidèle's programme this remarkable performance was to take the best part of an hour, with frequent pauses for refreshment and imprecation between shots.

At the third table everyone's favorite teen duo, Groundrat and Foundflat, were attempting to outdo each other with trick shots. Marie-Fidèle watched Foundflat successfully carry off a quadruple plant, then declaimed, 'The table is a metaphor for the class struggle. The pack of reds is the exploited proletariat whose extracted surplus value supports a parasitic ruling class of capitalists, which together with their class allies are represented by the coloured balls. In contrast to the indistinguishable proletarian reds these middle and upper class fractions are distinctly hierarchized from the yellow of petit-bourgeois lower management to the black of internationally mobile bankers. The unfolding of history according to the principles of historical materialism is revealed through the succession of pots, until finally only the black ball remains on the table, the stage of maximally condensed contradiction in which the apparent victory of the global ruling class of finance-capitalists is but a precondition of their final expropriation. For the white ball, which in itself is worth nothing, stands for the inexorably developing forces of production against which the relations of production are in class society always in conflict. But history is a dialectical process, the result of working through the material contradictions within the social formation, and therefore has no predetermined outcome. History's contradictions exist both within the social and the individual. Far from being merely the passive effects of a history outside their control, the exploited classes can, by acting on the understanding of their objective role, become the active agents of a consciously determined history. The rules are not fixed, however much they may seem to have the status of natural law. The point is not to interpret the game but to change it.'

Taking to Class War like UHT milk, no petit-bourgeois equivocation for them, Groundrat and Foundflat, in a historical discontinuity as unanticipated as 1917, came up with an entirely new version of snooker, in which the red balls were used to pot the colours, and once down they stayed down, while any reds accidentally pocketed were returned triumphant to the table. Finally only the white ball and the reds were left. Then, co-operatively not competitively, the task was to encircle the white ball until it could no longer be cued without striking a red, the point at which the productive forces were at last under the control of the producers, the point at which prehistory would end and history begin, the end of the game. What came next was a matter of debate, with Groundrat in favour of inventing yet another version, Foundflat opting for the original game which s/he insisted was more fun.

Without even bothering to stabilize the spell, so well had it taken, Marie-Fidèle concentrated her energies on the fourth and last table. The players, one thin to the point of emaciation, the other grosser than ever, were silhouetted against the grimy square of the hall's one window beyond which a faulty neon sign of a cheap hotel flashed intermittently. They seemed to be involved in an altercation about someone they referred to as the kid, with the fat man claiming he'd been as a son to him, while his companion sneeringly derided such an idea with the opinion he'd been nothing but a two bit gunsel. It seemed also they were sharing the cue of the deceased kid for reasons that were not entirely clear to Marie-Fidèle, since there was a full rack next to the table. It would have been hard to imagine less suitable candidates for Mother, her final spell, but even they must each have once had one.

Draining her tisane, Marie-Fidèle proposed, 'The table is the image of a woman. The initial layout of the balls, either this way

or the other

signifies the imaginary female object of male desire as an ideal of perfection against the ground of nature's green. The white cue ball comes successively under the control of the symbolically male players as a series of attacks are made on the idealized female figure, resulting finally in a table cleared of all balls except the white, which now emerges as the sign of the patriarchal right of sole possession of the mother. The course of the game symbolizes the passage from the object of desire, perfect yet threatening, to the mother, venerated yet subordinate, which is the fundamental ideological operation of patriarchal culture. Once complete the game can only begin again, in as infantile an attempt at mastery of the mother's absence as that of Freud's grandson throwing the cotton reel on its thread into the cot and endlessly retrieving it.'

At the spell's conclusion the thin player was leaning over the table cueing up for his shot. Without warning he jerked upright, stood rigid and sightless for perhaps five seconds, then folded to the floor in a foetal position clutching one of the table legs with his arms. Instead of going to his aid the fat player seized the cue from his nerveless fingers and heaving his belly up over the cushion hit the cue ball with dramatic force the full length of the table to smash a red into the far end pocket. In quick succession and with escalating violence he potted the pink, then another red, scattering the dozen left in the pack in all directions, then the black, which thumped into the back of the pocket with such velocity that it leapt clear of the leather restraining rim and curved through the air to hit the floor three metres away. Whereupon the fat man burst into tears and slumped, blubbering inconsolably, on the surface of the table.

Somewhat startled at the unexpected effects of Mother, Marie-Fidèle nevertheless fed a stabilizing series into the calculator to maintain it. Having come this far, she figured, it would be wrong to abandon the experiment for sentimental reasons. Besides, none of the players would have any subsequent recollections of their experiences. All four spells were now operational. What she had to do now, if her nerve held, was to lift the quarantine that was preventing each spilling over beyond the psychic field of its carriers.

Filling her lungs Marie-Fidèle with a great shout released a word that had never before been spoken, that had up to this time existed only as writing.

Nothing whatsoever happened. Or rather, everyone in the hall began to return to their condition before she had begun her magic. Pair by pair, the players were reverting to their previous states and styles of play. The high-minded gentlemen became once more low-browed snooker bruisers, the Newtonian-existentialists were again two Irishmen on a spree, Groundrat and Foundflat forgot revolution for massé shots, and the mother-loving, mother-hating noir villains went back to mourning the missing member of their trio. All, it seemed, had been in vain.

In a multiply-reinforced bunker deep below the ridge of hills to the east of our city, a certain high level military commander was poised over a snooker table, about to take his shot. It had not been an easy day. He had a lot of things on his mind. The moral responsibility of knowing you're the one to give the command to launch the missiles that will take out 117 Soviet land-based targets, the majority of them within heat and blast range of cities, was not a comfortable burden, and with increasing international tension he had been examining his conscience as never before. 117 warheads, attached to missiles whose pre-programmed flight paths, perfect trajectories subject only to the laws of physics, with a calculated accuracy on strike of less than one hundred metres, to be sent on their way by his choice, his sole free anguished choice. He understood even better than the politicians that Marx was right in supposing that the motor of history was the class struggle, and international politics was no exception. He thought of his grandfather, not someone he spoke of in the top brass mess, who'd been on strike in 1926 when those of his fellow officers had been busy breaking it. He thought of his mother, how lovely she'd been when he was a boy, and how they'd gone for walks together through the windswept hills and valleys not so far from where he was now stationed, countryside he still loved more than any other.

As this officer cued up to take his shot, these various thoughts and memories converged in his mind as if a barrier separating them had been removed. Together they had implications none of them had ever had separately, implications that brought him out in a film of sweat as he understood what had to be done. When the frame finished he begged off any further play on grounds of tiredness. But instead of going to his quarters he descended two levels of the underground complex to the computing centre. At a console he

79

called up a programme that he had monitored in conjunction with the systems analysts and programmers. Feeding in his top security operator's code he made a series of small changes to certain subroutines, then, backtracking through the entry protocols, deleted any possibility that his alterations could be detected without wiping the whole programme. Finally, he inserted a standard enquiry to account for the fact he had had access to the computer. Back in his quarters he poured himself a large whisky, which he slowly sipped while reading a few pages of his book before going to bed.

In the snooker hall, Marie-Fidèle said to the barkeep, 'I think I'll have that drink you're always wanting me to try.'

Happily the barkeep went to work with his cocktail shaker. Some gin, some vodka, freshly squeezed mango juice, a dash of grenadine, a squeeze of lemon, the white of an egg, all shaken together over cracked ice and poured into a sugar-frosted glass.

Four

Fish figure once in North By Northwest, an otherwise land-locked movie. As the train heading west skirts a lake by the track, Roger O. Thornhill, fugitive from the law for a murder he hasn't committed, takes the only place left in the dining car opposite a young women whom he asks what she recommends from the menu. She replies, 'I had the brook trout – a bit trouty, but quite nice', words whose intonation sent sales soaring in our city as cinephile gourmets searched for similarly flawed fish. Hooked, Thornhill orders.

From fish to introductions. She tells him she is Eve Kendall, an industrial designer, 'twenty six and unmarried, now you know everything', which he doesn't because she is a double agent working for the CIA, operating as the lover of the spy Vandamm who had mistaken Thornhill for the non-existent Kaplan concocted by the CIA to protect Eve's cover, and is also on the train in murderous pursuit of Thornhill. Eve, on the other hand, knows everything, and seeing the police board the train as it makes an unscheduled stop, offers him the sanctuary of her compartment, 3901. Already the element thirteen, as well as the decoy Kaplan, is fully in play. Eve's age, the first two digits of her compartment number, its sum of digits, as also that of Kaplan's room number, 436, at the Hotel Ambassador, New York City, unobtrusively signal towards the film's precursor, made by the same director in another country, The Thirty Nine Steps. Such arbitary signs and their recurrence, muses a critic in the back row of the audience.

Something Eve doesn't know is the significance of the O in the initials R. O. T. on the book of matches in Thornhill's hand. 'Nothing', he replies, and cheerfully acknowledges the acronym ROT. The back row critic notes the substitutory ring ROT, JOT, JOB, ROB, ROT, along with RON and ROCK all good presidential material, no doubt. The match-book returns in the showdown at the end, when Eve, in mortal danger from Vandamm who has learned of her true allegiance, is warned by Thornhill's scribbled message on the inside cover as she waits to fly out secretly with Vandamm for an unstated foreign destination. She makes to escape on the pretext of a lost earring, but the film further delays its resolution. Tension must be heightened to the limit of endurance before it is released, a transition achieved in the climactic metonymy of the dissolve from Thornhill's hand reaching down to where Eve hangs by her fingertips on the vertical cliff-face of Mount Rushmore, with its four presidential countenances, to his lifting her up on to the top bunk of the train speeding back east – hope of renascent capitalism – followed by the terminal metaphor of the train entering a tunnel whistling, a heterosexual triumphalism that may be undercut by the topology of the torus, which the tunnel undeniably is unless they're heading for an unexpected crash. Or crack, the wiseacre in the back row murmurs.

From private jokes to cruel cuts. Eve makes her appearance one third of the way through the film, the identical place where Marion, in Hitchcock's subsequent Psycho, is multiply stabbed to death while naked under a shower, in a scene of renowned technical virtuosity. The alliance of sexuality and death is also evident in the scene in North by Northwest where Thornhill, in compartment 3901, encircles Eve's neck with his hands. A triple torus come to think of it, thinks the alert spectator. Their dialogue runs:

Eve 'Maybe you're planning on murdering me. Right here. Tonight.'

Thornhill 'Shall I?'

Eve 'Please do.'

As they kiss the camera cuts back and forth from Cary Grant's grey close-cropped head to Eve Marie-Saint's glossy platinum blond, their faces alternating, the classic system of shot reverse shot.

Critic 'How deeply charged the terminology of cinema is with the vocabulary of war.'

Her companion 'How deeply entrenched is the assumption of mutual attraction between young woman and older man. He must be twice her age.'

A third voice 'Some people want to watch the film, if you don't mind.'

Back and forth the couple fact/fiction repeats the palindromic name of the actress in that of the character. Equally, the palindromic doubling recurs with the talkative back row duo, Anna both.

Eve, meanwhile, is merely pretending to fall for Thornhill, in order to keep him under surveillance for Vandamm, in order to keep Vandamm under surveillance for the CIA. The series of baffles deployed by Hitchcock to bifurcate the knowledge of the characters in the film and that of the audience trying to watch it here takes the form of the double doubt: the spectator imagines Thornhill's trust in Eve is misplaced, while in the end it is entirely appropriate. What has faded from view is Eve's loyalty to the State, personified by the Professor, head of the CIA, played with grim relish by Leo G. Carroll. 'War is hell, Mr Thornhill,' he says, as Thornhill deplores the way the agency has treated Eve as dispensable, 'even when it's a cold one.' When Thornhill comments that maybe they ought to start losing a few cold wars, he morosely rejoins, 'We're already doing that.' Eve and Thornhill's deepening feelings for each other are expressed in a tender confessional scene in sunlit pinewoods which Hitchcock had to fight the studio to retain, when they meet up for what she supposes to be the last time and he imagines to be the beginning of their life together. But before this can occur Eve must carry out her patriotic duty, thereby atoning for her sexual promiscuity and for having taken Vandamm as a lover. Only then can she be rescued by Thornhill from the peril her honour has placed her in, and become his wife. The narrative may conclude only after making its sacrificial offerings to the gods of prevailing opinion. Finally the macguffin, the empty sign around which the plot revolves, here a roll of microfilm, reaches its morally pre-ordained destination.

After being spoken of by the Professor, the microfilm of 'government secrets', like Eve, makes its appearance under cover, at an auction that Thornhill disrupts in order to secure his escape from Vandamm's henchmen. As Vandamm bids for the pre-Columbian American sculpture, Thornhill cries out, 'It's a fake', not knowing that it really is, being the secret container for the secret microfilm. Once again Thornhill proves himself the speaker of the truth when least suspecting that he is doing so. He is the idiot savant, whose blunders disrupt an order in unstable equilibrium and reconstitute it as a stable one. The often-cited and celebrated crop-dusting sequence shows his madness in action, where by the end of it, having narrowly escaped death by decapitation, shooting, asphyxiation, impact, and fire, he leaves behind him, as music erupts for the first time since the menacing diagonal of the long straight road across the prairie opened the scene, an exploded petrol tanker, a crashed plane, and an irate farmer robbed of his pick-up truck, all to permit him discover that Eve has sold him down the river. He's wrong again. There are no rivers in North By Northwest.

Five

Thirteen skydivers fall from the height of the Jungfrau, out of the plane on the command of the jumpmaster, to stabilize into a whistling ellipsoid as gravity is countered by an equal and opposite wind. They extend arms and legs, spreadeagled on the rack of air. The cluster converges, flattens, with limbs made ailerons giving each control. Below the ground's an indifferent wall of indecipherable signs, a map with no writing on it, while above, just a matter of pulling in an arm to flip the world around, the sky's an achingly perfect blue, across which the contrail of the plane is already blurring into imprecision. The training justified, the hectoring of the jumpmaster silenced, they exult in the composite sensations of speed and rest, one then the other, as undecidable as the this way or that way of a cube diagrammed on a page. The surface dwellers have given themselves over to levity, the two crushed dimensions of everyday existence foreclosed in the ecstasy of the third.

Time's running down, the time to do what this jump's all about. They've been working through the twenty-six letters of the alphabet, S/Z last Sunday, and now's the climax of the season, the only two left to do, Y and X.

For technical reasons concerning the ease of transition from one to the other, Y comes first. The disc of divers, legs together, arms apart, separates into three lines of four, angled at 120°, centred on the thirteenth, so:

At the top right is Miranda, next to her is Candida, then Emma, then Dorothea, with Anna in the centre; below Anna is Virginia, followed by Livia, Margherita and Rebecca; top left is Clea, then Ada, Oedipa, and joining hands with Anna to complete the figure is Ariadne.

Suburbanites all, except for the inveterate city-dweller Ariadne, they do this every Sunday afternoon, weather permitting, over an airfield to the west of our city. What they get out of it is a mystery to their husbands and boyfriends, who secretly worry each time there's a jump. To the women there's nothing like it, this free fall coupled with control, and beyond that there's something else, which they aver to only jokingly as they clamber into the rattletrap of a plane or as they shower together afterwards, the impulse to carry on down, to plunge earthwards ripcord ignored, emergency canopy refused, to smash into the ground, bones splintering, organs bursting, in a terminal impact of their bodies on to that of the planet. Against this wish the figures they between them make assert something, they're not quite sure what.

Dorothea and Virginia release their grip on Anna and re-attach themselves to Ariadne, while Miranda and Rebecca cast off from the end of their lines and fly inwards so that Miranda catches hold of Anna and Rebecca clasps Miranda, and those already in place adjust the angles between the bisecting lines to 90°. Legs apart, arms apart, they achieve their

```
        X           X
          X       X
            X   X
              X
            X   X
          X       X
        X           X
```

On the ground the spectators cheer and clap. They sigh with relief as the canopies begin to open, four, pause, another four, pause, three more, then one, and after an eternity of expectation, only one. Beneath the dozen orange canopies seemingly motionless there's an object falling. Let it be someone else, silently screams each watcher, head tilted back, eyes screened against the glare, certain that it's not. Whereabouts did she come from? Not any of the four at the ends, Clea, Candida, Rebecca, Margherita, their chutes clearly opened, didn't they? Nor the next wave, Ada, Emma, Miranda, Livia, surely? She's still going down, the second chute's failed to open. It wasn't Oedipa, someone's loving gaze was fixed on her throughout, wasn't it? Nor Dorothea, nor Virginia likewise, right? Six seconds for a thousand feet and she's no more than a thousand feet up, falling ever faster. Either Anna or Ariadne, which is it? The spectators race towards the perimeter of the field, towards the brightly-coloured shape on the dull, black tarmac, like the letter Y, like the letter X, in a child's alphabet.

Six

From the word go, Sara was definite that this holiday she would be by herself. No company. She took the Professor's advice on location, renting at a special departmental rate her weekend cottage in the Forêt de la Double, a neck of the woods she was assured would give her all the peace and quiet she needed. And only a short drive from the lovely river Dordogne and a slightly longer one to the inimitable caves at Lascaut. After such a pressured year, what with the cuts and everything, she needed to get away from it all and collect herself.

So, she said to herself, as she set out in her orange Volkswagen, packed with paraphernalia, never forgetting her typewriter and a box of Croxley script filched from the department supply, it would be Sara Bella and the Whole Hog.

She was determined when there to write, not her usual stuff for the learned journals, but the 'real thing'. The real thing: freedom to say whatever she wanted, to be torn up or offered to the reading public as the fancy took her. Two months in the long vacation, a cottage with thick whitewashed walls, cool stone floors, geraniums in pots outside. If she couldn't write there where could she?

The weather, naturally, was perfect – misty early mornings with the dew beaded along the threads of spiders' webs crisscrossing the vines shading the verandah, hot days humming with insects, warm thick purple evenings when nightjars silently flew past her open door in pursuit of moths.

It would take a day or two, she appreciated, to settle down, get the hang of the local markets, make the acquaintance of the farmer whose land the cottage was on, prospect the nearby restaurant. She didn't want to be a recluse, just alone. The day or two somehow turned into a week, there being problems like a leaky tap and noisy tappets, both fixed affably but slowly to the benefit of her French. At last, stocked up for the 14 juillet long weekend with bread, cheese, saucisson, yoghurt, salad, plenty of fruit (the influence of Groundrat and Foundflat), she was truly ready to begin.

At which point she discovered two things. One was her block, the other was ?? The block hit her with the force of a sledgehammer, ?? was more subtle.

As she sat down, a glass of Perrier at her side, the typewriter shaded by the overhanging vines, ready to write to the limits of what she'd felt, thought, experienced – in short 'the truth' – a terrible lassitude descended upon her, an inexpressible weariness that had her yawning like she'd missed a night's sleep rather than had an unbroken eight hours. She decided to make a cup of coffee to sharpen herself up. With it bubbling up into the top of the jug she felt enlivened already, and made her way back to the table with fresh resolve. Once there, though, the tiredness came over her again, and the coffee only made her feel edgy and irritable on top of it all. She decided to go for a walk.

Setting off down the trail into the forest she quickly left behind such few sounds of human presence as there were at the cottage, the odd car perhaps and the steady chug of Pierre's diesel engine pumping water into the lake he kept for his geese. As she walked the tension generated by her block gradually eased, and she felt that the afternoon might turn out to be productive after all. It was a matter of finding a suitable form for the ideas in her head. She had somehow to transform them, work them over, otherwise they'd be banal and of no interest to anyone. It was a bit like off-centre retinal images, she decided. If you tried to look at them directly, then they disappeared, only to reappear on the margins of vision. Enthused by her metaphor she made to turn back, have a bite of lunch and then get to work.

Whereupon she found that the track she'd been following was no more. Either it had petered out and she'd not noticed, having been so immersed in the problems of her block, or else she had strayed from it. Either way she was surrounded by a mass of trees. And although the sun could be made out through the canopy, giving her an approximate south, she had no idea in which direction she should head back. She was lost in the forest – as symbolic an eventuality as she could have wished for, and one she'd have otherwise quite relished. But her ideas now were abundant and articulated, begging to be put on to paper.

She was about to set a course at random by the sun and keep to it, on the supposition she'd come to a road sooner or later, when she noticed some scattered fragments of fungus near the bole of a massive oak. Something about them jogged a memory, and she stooped to investigate further. Picking a morsel up, she noted its dark, shiny, black surface where it had been broken, in contrast to the dusty grey exterior. The scent, when she placed it to her nose, was extraordinary, and it could only mean one thing. She had heard Pierre talk of truffles, and how the very best pâté de foie gras would have a core of black truffle, though his own product malheureusement fell short of the quality that would have been worthy of such an addition. While she was in principle doubtful about the morality of forcefeeding geese, and personally found the instrument used to do so revolting, with its long nozzle and capacious bowl to take the greasy maize, she also respected the local culture, with an economy largely based upon the practice. The idea of truffles, though, was altogether more appealing, even if their price was affordable only to the upper bourgeoisie. What she liked especially was the fact that they were also the favourite delicacy of wild boar, which Pierre said had once roamed these woods. Since their departure many years ago, truffles had become a rarity and truffle-hunting had died out.

But these were surely truffles, or at least fragments of them, which meant that someone or something had unearthed them from the soil where they grew parasitically upon oak roots. The fact that there were still traces scattered suggested that it hadn't been human agency, not with truffles worth hundreds of francs a kilo.

Picking up some of the larger fragments to give to Sandrine back at the farm, Sara noticed a further patch of disturbed ground a little further on. And when she reached it, with its traces of truffle, she saw another, and beyond it another. With less concern now for the traces themselves than for whatever it was causing them, Sara quickly moved from one patch of disturbed ground to the next. The trail she followed wove through the trees, meandering only to follow the easiest contours of the gently undulating land. It seemed to be leading somewhere, as if there were a guiding purpose. With mounting excitement, linked to a kind of apprehensive fearfulness, she noticed that the traces were becoming fresher. The newly turned earth smelt damp, not having had time to dry off in the sunshine filtering through the canopy, and the truffle fragments themselves exuded an increasingly strong and alluring odour. There was also another smell wafting disturbingly from the exposed roots, which she could only describe as animal. This new smell, she couldn't decide if she liked it or not, but it was certainly unlike anything she'd encountered before. It seemed composed equally of bestial savagery and transcendent joy, though how such abstractions could possibly smell of anything she fully appreciated. Soon the scent was augmented by faint sounds that grew in volume as she pushed forward through the thickening underbrush. Her line of sight was now reduced to a few paces, only opening up to give her glimpses of the next patch of earth and its abandoned cargo of fungus. But she could have followed whatever it was blindfold, by scent and hearing. Above the crashing sounds coming from just beyond the thicket, she could also hear a grunting and snorting, that had her oblivious of danger pushing forward towards its origin.

Suddenly the brush gave way to a clearing, dappled by sunlight, through which fritillaries fluttered and dragonflies danced. In the centre of the glade, gouging the earth with its tusks, stood an enormous wild boar. Its massive, grey head turned as she burst from the bushes. Its little eyes converged upon her.

At which point the space-time structure around and including Sara faulted.

In the first continuation, Sara summoned up her martial energies precisely as the whole hog acquired a demeanour that could mean only one thing. With its tail stiffly erect, its jaws dripping saliva, its eyes blazing its intent, it began its charge across the glade. The nearest tree with branches low enough to reach was across the clearing, and behind her brambles barred her path. Her only chance lay in a weapon, preferably a high velocity armour-piercing gun, but anything, she prayed, would do. Whether the spirits that haunt the caves of Lascaut beneath the hills to the east of the forest drew upon their collective wisdom in the art of killing creatures stronger than yourself, or whether the metallurgical knowhow saturating the Mediterranean from Toledo to Crete forged it in the temporal gate afforded by the space-time slippage, or whether a pique-niqueur/euse had left behind the wherewithall for opening that can of sardines with no key, or through any one of an infinite number of other explanations of varying plausibility, there landed in Sara's outstretched hand a sword, bright, sharp and lethal. The hog's head alone was nearly a metre wide, fronted by a mass of bristle as impenetrable as coconut matting, with an occiput thick enough to splinter a mallet. Only through its eyes, tiny and red, was it vulnerable. It was almost upon her. With the courage of a matador, with the precision of a surgeon, Sara stepped to one side and plunged her raised sword downwards through its left eye, deep into the beast's brain. The force of its charge snapped the blade clear off, spraining her wrist as the sword twisted in her hand. The forward momentum slowed, with its trotters scattering turf. It turned, coughing, to renew the assault, but already synapses were disarticulating, blood was flooding its cranium in a massive haemorrhage. It took several unsteady steps, then veered off course and rolled over on to its side. There followed, in succession, a sighing belch, a convulsive defecation, a spasm that shook its entire frame, and a slight, almost tentative movement of one foot. It was dead. Flinging her broken sword down next to the corpse on which the first flies were settling, Sara ran from the glade, ran through the maze of the forest, unaware that without the truffle traces to guide her she was unerringly following another trail, laid down by myriad spiders, the thread of whose webs led through the trees in a shimmering, gossamer text, drawing her back to her cottage where exhilarated she would fall upon her typewriter and tell it like it was, down to the last fantastic detail, her block blasted to kingdom come.

In the second continuation, Sara summoned up her erotic energies precisely as the whole hog acquired a demeanour that could mean only one thing. With its tail stiffly erect, its jaws dripping saliva, its eyes blazing its intent, it began its charge across the glade. It really was a magnificent creature, perfectly adapted to its environment, a specimen of extraordinarily balanced and harmonious proportions. She especially like the way its tusks curved up from its bristly jaw to overlap in front of its highly intelligent eyes. With its noble head, so ponderously steady on deep muscular shoulders, its body tapering towards thighs rippling with fitness, those delicate four feet and their neat little cloven hooves, what a delight it was. And those grizzled bristles, what a measure of maturity, of experience! No wonder she had been drawn here from the outset! It knew how to live, this hog, its enjoyment of truffles just the beginning of its capacity for pleasure. But wait, what's this?, it's undergoing a transformation, from beast, would you believe, to man. And – not just any man, but the trimmest 39-for-ever-year-old as took a siesta in a wood in southwestern France after a morning spent hunting truffles and woke up a werehog, the effect it must be acknowledged of a spell cast by his cast-off Marie-Fidèle, something of a charmeuse and a bit of a comédienne, who hails from these parts and decided to get her own back. Yes, folks, it was Gropius, taking two weeks off out of fifty-two. Clad modestly in a towel, he said, Surely, hadn't they met somewhere before. And Sara, recollecting, said, Yes they had, back in our city, wasn't this a coincidence. What's more, his orange Volkswagen was parked just down the track, and if she needed a lift anywhere he'd by only too happy to oblige. So Sara arrived in some style back at her cottage, where she said, Why didn't he come in, join her for dinner, she could rustle something up. And he said, How about truffles in cream for starters. After truffles they couldn't go far wrong, and didn't. During the days following Gropius lazed around reading, Sara pounded on her typewriter, inventing like crazy, her block dissolved in aqua regia.

It would do for a first draft.

Of course their names would have to be changed, that went without saying. And Pierre and Sandrine worried her, a feeling she's lifted them from somewhere else, but she couldn't put her finger on what. There were other details too. While 'tap. . . tappets' had seemed fine when it came off the top of her head, it sounded rather contrived on re-reading. The blanks alongside the block, its residue she supposed, would need filling in with something or other. Two orange VWs was a plain error, of course, funny how she'd forgotten the first. More serious, she thought, were the stylistic inadequacies of the piece. It came from academic writing, this tendency towards Latinate sentences with their damned dependent clauses. And a word like 'whereupon' just had to go. There was also something very weird about the rest of the 'bestial savagery and transcendent joy' sentence, but she sort of liked it anyway. As for what it was all about, well, who knows, not for her to decide, though she thought she'd handled the shift from naturalism to the postmodernist double ending and magic realism with some adroitness for a beginner.

'Music?'

'Yes, put something on.'

'What?'

'You choose.'

The stately progression of Schubert's B Flat Trio carries on the balmy air through the lit window of the cottage, beyond the vine-covered verandah, to the woods where a sow and her litter are picking their way through the leaf debris, noses attuned to the aroma of the food they love.

Seven

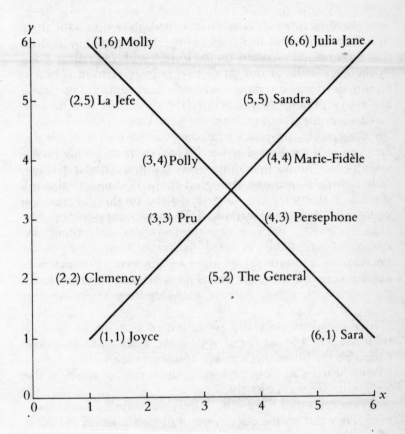

Eight

The word circulates, 'A woman is being sawn in half.' It is murmured in dental surgeries, whispered down long institutional corridors, repeated on the leather-upholstered couches in the great halls of our city's two railway termini. There's an urgency to its utterance that lends it credibility. Questions are asked: Where? Why? Who? By whom? At first no one can answer them, but gradually suggestions are forthcoming. 'In the circus', proposes someone, 'as part of a do-or-die farewell by a celebrated artiste.' 'No,' counters another, 'it's taking place on an operating table in a private hospital, her only chance, a slim one, though if anybody can carry this off it's Sir Wallaby Chase, surgeon to the mighty.' Proposals proliferate, fed by a current of inventive story-telling. No evidence exists, nothing concrete, nothing to ground the rumours, until a child is heard insisting it's happening now, on stage in a theatre given over to children's productions. For some reason or other this child is believed, and she leads the way back down narrow half-forgotten streets to the venue of the scene.

In the theatre only the accoutrements of the magician's trade are left: a wand, a red voile scarf, a saw with an oxidic patina on the blade. A caretaker confirms the child's account, having heard it all from backstage, those cries of agony as the act got under way, ghastly.

'Wasn't it a trick?' we ask. 'Surely this didn't actually happen? They put on the effects, you know, audiences like a bit of realism.'

But the caretaker remains adamant. When you've been around as long as he has you get to know the real McCoy, nothing illusory about what he'd heard. So we press the little girl for details, what exactly she witnessed.

The stage, it seems, was set for the star turn. A roll on a kettle-drum preceded the opening of the wine-red curtains on to a stage bare of props save a large, wooden box on legs. The magician himself, splendid in top hat and cape, entered from the right, spinning coloured handkerchiefs out of the air, waving his wand, to the ecstatic applause of the young audience packed into the theatre. Soon there were doves fluttering and rabbits scampering about him, as he found more and more of these creatures secreted about his person. Then a shower of money, notes and coin, poured from his sleeve, prompted by tickling his armpit with his wand. The children all found this hilarious, and even one or two of us suppressed a giggle at the telling of it. Their laughter changed to hushed expectancy when the magician clapped his hands and pointed his wand to the other side of the stage. In her silver-sequined swimsuit and fishnet tights she was as beautiful as could be imagined, tall, long-legged, with a confident stride and brilliant smile, and the children clapped until their hands were sore. Together the magician and his assistant did one or two tricks with knotted ropes, grownup tricks those and a bit boring, but then at last the climax of the performance came. The magician produced a fearsome saw from under his cape, tapping it with his wand to show it was no fake. The assistant, still smiling, climbed into the box and lay down so that her feet were projecting through two holes at one end and her head through a larger one at the other. When the assistant indicated she was ready, the magician lowered the lid of the box and locked it with a large key which he then swallowed, much to everyone's delight. Next, after another roll of the drum, he placed the saw at an angle in the middle of one of the long top edges of the box and began to move it back and forth, gently at first, then with increasing vigour. The rasping sound as it bit into the wood had the audience on the edge of their seats, watching with rapt attention as the pile of sawdust beneath the box grew and the blade cut deeper and deeper, nearer and nearer the figure inside. Soon there could be no doubt it must have reached her, but her smile remained in place, reassuring the young spectators that whatever was happening it couldn't be so terrible. Eventually, when the box and its contents were almost sawn through, just a half inch or so left to go, the magician threw down his instrument and, inserting his fingers into the line of the cut, wrenched the two halves apart. In the brief instant the interior was revealed, before the magician flung his cape over the divide, you could see, our little witness says, a multi-coloured confusion of organs. Even afterwards, visible beneath the cape, before the curtains came across to close the performance, blood dripped steadily on to the stage.

'I'll second that,' says the caretaker. 'After the show I mopped up the mess.' He'll show us, if we want, the stains on the boards and the traces of dried blood in the cracks between them.

We decline his offer, having heard enough already to accept the truth of the child's account. Our concern now is to establish a motive for the crime and to apprehend its perpetrator. Not least among the questions in need of answering is why the victim was so compliant in her mutilation. There is so little to go on. No address cards, no booking forms, nor prior registration of the act with the appropriate committee, indeed none of the civic supports one might have expected for a performance of this kind. Nor is there any trace of the body, although our redoubtable Chief of Police has personally taken over the interrogation of suspects in the expectation that someone may remember something for him they'd otherwise be inclined to forget. Nobody has talked, or if they have it is deemed inconsequential. We are all at a loss. We are waiting for someone or something to break.

Now rumours are surfacing of strange events in other quarters, incidents that in themselves signify nothing but taken together are surely meaningful.

From our city art gallery comes the news of a bizarre act of vandalism. Two paintings have been desecrated, one a Victorian High Renaissance mermaid, the other a recently acquired Magritte (or a good copy of it), which the explanatory gloss alongside refers to as 'a real man's mermaid', depicting a figure whose upper half is fish and lower is woman. These two have each been cut along the join of woman and fish, and the pieces reassembled with paste and staples into a semblance of entire fish and entire woman. The results have caused an outcry among our city's art critics, with one going into print saying the defiler deserves a punishment to fit the crime, viz. quartering.

Then there is the story from a snooker club near the docks, where the cloth of just one of the four tables has been slit with geometrical precision down its long axis. Even stranger is the fact that it was then sewn up, with a fine cross-stitch, but with the edges of the cloth slightly displaced longitudinally, so that the central line of spots forms a series of tangential semicircles.

News too from another club, Fêng's in Chinatown, where the sealed and chilled packs of cards for yesterday's tournament were found, when opened, to have been tampered with. All court cards had been cut neatly across the middle to form identical halves, from which new whole cards had been pasted together on an apparently random basis: jack with queen, queen with king, king with jack, as well as the original unities, but always within the correct suit. Mr Fêng himself is of the opinion that this bears the signature of the Triads, but we are not so sure.

Rather more in the public eye has been the series of errors, as the Union insists they are, appearing on page one of our city's tabloid, the Moon. Extraordinary things are happening to the Moongirls. One morning it was Sonia, whose poses with beachballs are legendary, shown in the regulation monokini, but with one breast detached from her body and reversed so the nipple lodged between her glossy, pouting, parted lips. Sonia's mother threatened to sue and was only persuaded to accept a substantial out-of-court settlement after a lengthy person-to-person call from the owner on his Caribbean island. Then Wendy, a favourite with Moonmen, appeared with her right leg missing, in its place what a perceptive reader would have noted was a goal post. Sure enough, on page twenty-four, Shot Of The Week was sizzling between a never-saw-it-coming keeper and Wendy's leg. Most contentious of all was the Saturday edition, which had the Moongirls demonstrating solidarity in front of the TV cameras and provided ammunition for campaigners of all persuasions. Gloria's lovely, headless body lay stretched luxuriantly across the page, perfect in every way but one. Nor was her head subsequently found, though a competition was inaugurated, first prize a week in the Seychelles with herself, to spot it lurking on the unsuspecting shoulders of anyone anywhere else in the Moon. Following this, Gloria has announced she is to become a newsreader on television, a profession where they take you seriously, and every print of every girl is scrutinized by a panel of experts before publication.

In the midst of everything, the little girl whose story began it all tells her mother that she was mistaken, then, under questioning, that she had made it all up, having supported her story by pouring a carton of blood bought at a pork butcher's over the stage. She weeps in repentance at having done such an awful thing.

Thereafter, sure enough, life gets back to normal. No more decapitations, defilements or defacements. Everyone breathes a sigh of relief, if a slightly regretful one.

What the little girl now confides to her younger sister, sworn to a pact of secrecy that she'd rather give her life for than betray, is that the first story was the true one, the second the invention. She really did see the magician's assistant chopped in two, and blood spurt, and her insides glisten, and the magician wipe his saw on his sleeve as he wheeled out the two pieces, one with her face still smiling, the other with her feet pointing heavenwards. 'We know one thing', says the little girl to her sister Katy, 'let them believe something else.'

Nine

Between heaven, across which a light aircraft slowly droned, and earth, tussocky upland grass blown by the breeze, Clemency Black stood black in her wetsuit. Her presence was noted by the yellow rectangular-pupilled eyes of sheep grazing a few yards away, by the skydivers in the plane, and by a party of walkers silhouetted on a ridge to the southeast. A lapwing tossed itself into the air, then tumbled calling to its hidden nest; a vole burrowed through the humus; ants swarmed. Life was a film spread thinly over rock sedimented and compressed by the accumulation of the dead bodies of sea-swimming creatures. The chances that Clemency should be alive at all were very slim, given her forty-two years against the billions preceding her birth. In taking up the challenge of her first pot, to call this once Gerald's macho bluff, she had not anticipated such a degree of loathing, bordering on panic, that confronted her now. He had disappeared into the hillside with a glance back over his shoulder that said it all. A greater terror took hold of her, that she might be what his condescending gaze implied she was, in her terms not god forbid his, a person who couldn't confront her darkest fantasies. The rope attaching them tugged at her waist. She switched on her helmet light and stepped down into the darkness.

Blind. Can't breathe. Help!

Sssssh. Calm, relax. Better.

Much better.

Ah so. Interface more than boundary life/death, seems to have affected inner speech, yet to find out what else.

Psi powers, always convinced had them, greatly enhanced. Premier insight: Gerald mucho scared macho muchacho, big need to overcome confinement phobia, hence caving fetish. Follows drive to prove at expense of others, will therefore push novice in hope of plea for respite, thus ego-mission accomplished.

Insight dispels residual fear. Pardon honorific leader, battle-of-wills game ended.

Am beginning to like rock: smooth cold texture, shades of grey to yellow, striation. Only unaesthetic input comes from sweating figure in front, odours of fear, combativeness wafting from wetsuit.

Passage meandering, incline maybe ten degrees down, floor even except for a few large boulders, roof variable height, up to five metres down to two. Arms out, can touch both sides: recall running down ginney as child, fingertips brushing layered vertical planks of fences, tingling sensation in fingers caused by vibration. Pleasure in repetition.

Gerald turns, detecting unseemly levity, mouths oafish phrase of encouragement/putdown which primary defences deflect on to rock, sorry Rock, and so don't even tangle with sense of it. Beam at baffled Gerald, Fun uh? Evidently earlier judgement on end of gameplay premature, some resentment yet to work out on hapless creature.

As for rock, apology has released flood of associations. First, Rock – river? – Hudson, youthful-folly heartthrob, even older-wiser Clem could have trouble keeping hands off of, like Jane Wyman her doe-eyed gardener in All That Heaven Allows. Dropping my ks, habit until speech-therapist got to work, come up with Pat Roc, mummy's favourite lady-actress; and greatest of feathered friends, roc in Sinbad. Therapy successful, ks returned, pink stick of rock of visit to BlackPool, and black pool in front, Gerald's in up to waist, now junior partner, haaagh, cold as cold sausage even through wetsuit, puzzling out how they got writing in. Grown in right places into original teenager, mummy's despair, just crazy 'bout Rock Around The Clock, disc/ movie, and dial of waterproof watch so described shows hour gone by already. Passage tilting up, river runs into rock, flood ends.

Gerald raises hand in agreed–upon signal: rest-time, choccy and dried fruit, swig from flasks refilled from torrent.

Map shows going about to get tricky, unless take softer option by-passing 500 metre crawl along horizontal chimney. Leader's saying one thing: Easier route right for beginners; thinking another: Like to show inferior female. So Led, into mischief, implies maybe he ought to, her having got through so far wetsuit gleaming: How about giving it a whirl? Pretends to ponder, does Gerald, while heart leaps at prospect of snivelling spouse needing rescue, and guess what, comfort leads to cuddles, cuddles lead to grateful saved unzipping wetsuit, etc, etc. Mumbles Gerald: If you think it's feasible. Sure, sure, goes Clem, blood up too, not quite sure why, though clear he's out to refute doubts re own self, overcome terrors to be found in tightest nooks, maybe even revenge for fact Clem's, after bearing boys, isn't.

Fed, watered, off we set. Soon time to bend, then crawl as tunnel becomes metre-high slit, roof and floor still converging. Now flat on tums, knees up pushing back, haven't done this for a while, hands slicking along polished floor, elbows pressure points exerting leverage to ease body forward. Slow progress, hard work, but sort of nice. Call out: How's it going up there? Grunts for answer. Hear him thinking: Easier for her, smaller than me. Transmit back: Forgotten tits.

Actually, tits feel great. Feels as if squeezed by huge gentle hand, body like toothpaste oozing out of tube. More pressure top and bottom as cleft gets even narrower.

Sudden revelation: of course, makes sense of terror/pleasure, repetition of birth trauma. So obvious what it's about, this crawling down into great-mother earth, am shamed by slow-wittedness, wonder if bearded figure seated at couch-head can forgive time-wasting. Push hard mummy, easy squeeze me, coming through, not far now, all for being born/reborn, cry ready for first breath in new world. Clem's own babies came easy, no pain just massive motion as if whole body organ for delivery of infant, ripe juicy fruit splitting open to yield up seed. Babies now grown men, bearded, moustached, both happy looking for original womb, no rush to find it, no complaints if they did. Recall their first cries upon entry/re-entry into world-not-of-their-own-choosing: no joke, uh? Sounded like, sounds like, cries from Gerald.

Whatsis? Is such a thing possible? Yes it is. Seems like Gerald's jammed.

Bye Gerald.

Joke? Only just.

Thing is to free arm stuck awkwardly, get him turned around. Standard breech delivery problem, except not mid-wife. Lots of noisy advice from immobile person to mobile person, until tell him: Shut up and do what told. Wonder: Is lubricating jelly part of caver's kit? Conclude: Must be

103

method involving yogic unfreeing of locked skeletal/muscular blockage. So, hyperventilate, get haemoglobin oxygenated. Now, slide/push, don't-think-feel philosophy here ultra-relevant, do believe we're moving. Oof! Distinct faecal smell assails nostrils. Wunderbar. Gerald in exertion/panic has fouled wetsuit. No change of nappies here, no powdered botty and creamy willy, you live with it fella. One last effort. And, Out!

Points to rent in wetsuit, explanation for master-race failure, matter of scag on rock hooking on to most crucial vulnerable part of corpus. Could have happened to anyone, says rescued. But didn't, says rescuer. Two world-systems at odds here, no resolution forthcoming. Silence falls.

But more to come, best part.

Next hour spent tracking along beaten paths. One cavern where torches reveal roof ten metres high, sharp stalactites, blobby stalagmites, destined to rendezvous a million years from now. Terrific, but clock-conscious Gerald says no loitering. With intent? Naughty thought of congress with tempting little stalagmite, but don't think spectator would approve. Some other time, you rude boy.

Frown creases Olympian's brow.

What's up Doc? Haven't even seen half these movies flying like Vampyr around head, getting in Hair. Go caving, what do you expect?

Seems like, hard to accept but facts are facts, there's a fork here not shown on map.

Wow! Original discovery. Fame at last. What luck.

Debate what to do next. Route as planned would go straight on, no more than half hour until emergence on far side of ridge of hills. If so, then should note point where it opens up, return some other time. Or could, intuitive female preference this, at least make tentative exploration now. All sorts of reasons why latter course inappropriate, needless to say. So play card: we go down there and Clem says nothing about humiliating rescue, okay? Reluctantly, Okay, but any complications, return immediately.

So off we set, orthodox him-in-front her-behind, gradual then steep descent. Torches reveal nothing special to untrained eye, roof just above head height, wide enough to let two pass comfortably, steps in steepest places. Must have done down three flights of them before implications broke through crust of idiocy in place of brain.

Steps?!!?

Hey, Gerald!

Oh ho, leader's getting own back: supercilious, Didn't think it worthwhile mentioning, so obvious, even to meanest intelligence, that passage manmade.

Let sexism pass, so mortified by lack of perception.

But, Who? Why? What? Questions for astute reader of geological substrata, knowing not all passages are natural.

Answers forthcoming just around next bend. Before that, practical question: How deep? Reply in punitive jargon, but gist is way way below floor of valley.

Curving round bend, through 180°, orientation reversed from SSE to NNW, and suddenly it's all signs, signs, signs, in rows, in columns, with Clem trying to make sense of them. Only sign missing is one of Gerald, who's vanished.

Inscribed on a door.

Grey metal, thick as hell is immediate intuition, radiation-proof, bomb-proof, certainly caver-proof, and no handle except an eight-spoked wheel in the middle of it. Try turning it left, right, won't budge. Evidently door not meant to be opened from outside, or else only by those with key. But no keyhole. And still no Gerald.

Turn attention to script. Seems to be arranged in crossword fashion, interlocking across and down. But this is odd, also perspective effect of third dimension inwards/outwards, maybe issue of special 3-D specs to read it. And, who knows, given right spectacles, all dimensions up to eleven here inscribed, trace of Big Bang, now compressed into neat Einsteinian four, whispering to Clem across aeons from original nanosecond of whoomph.

Anyhow, cosmology apart, script in many tongues, veritable Babel babbling silently to mouth-agape reader: American, French, Soviet-Cyrillic, Hindi/Sindi, you bet Mandarin, before Clem's acquantance conks out.

Couldn't rule out non-terrestrial languages represented here too.

Holy shit!

Starting to feel choccy-bar's about to exit from queasy tum.

And where's Gerald?

There you are. Is Clem pleased to see him/you. Where you/he been?

Well, turns out smart Gerald's been back counting steps. Three flights, like unconsciously descended. Each of thirteen. Three times thirteen, thirteen times three, is commutable.

World champ thicko Clem gets it. Exults: The Thirty Nine Steps.

P.S. Original or remake?

P.P.S. What's the difference?

Howls of protest caver movie-buffs.

Time to return to surface, light, fresh air. Gerald and Clem, reconciled pro tem, doubt for long, but nice while it lasts, clamber back up.

Lots to ponder: powers, principalities, possibility of paranoia.

The two potholers, Clemency Black first, followed by her husband, emerged from the earth into the valley adjacent to that they had set out from. Their presence was noted by a flock of sheep which had drifted over the fell in search of fresh pasture, by some skydivers in the small plane circling the blue dome of heaven above, and by a party of walkers silhouetted on the northwesterly skyline.

Ten

At dawn, with the frosts deliquescing off the steppe in spectres that imaged those of our nightmares, we would line up along the banks of the Ussuri River, and through loud-hailers would address the invaders on the other side, and they would also line up and shout back their abusive lies, while the sun dispersed the mists and turned the interminable steppe from palest azure to gold, and dawn's chill gave way to the all-too-brief cool of the middle morning before the noon sun poured fire down upon us, and the subtleties of our first challenges would be replaced by an unreasoning invective that knew no limits and would thicken the shimmering heat, while the great waters of the Ussuri rolled past between us and them, until at last we would retire to tend to the wounded and carry on the immemorial tasks of border guards, the counting of ordnance, calculation of dues, revision of protocols, peeling vegetables.

That day the opening salvoes were Political Economy, and Female Relatives Excluding Mothers.

So,

> O soldiers of the Union of Soviet Socialist Republics, do you eat caviare like your Politburo on your generous pay, or do you make do with grey bread leavened with chalk dust?
>
> Your so-called Revolution, peasants and proletarians, deposed the Czar only to recrown him as Comrade.
>
> Listen, you Turkmens, Uzbeks, Kazahks, Latvians, Mongols, Armenians, Estonians, Ukrainians and other nationalities, how many of your countrymen exercise power behind the Kremlin walls?
>
> Usurpers, interlopers, the land you stand on was stolen by the Czars. Cuckoo, cuckoo.

Varying our aim we let fly with,

> Remember the dog you gave your wife to console her during your absence? Rumour has it she no longer wants her husband back.
>
> Your grandmother's cooking was famous for versts

around. If you wanted to be rid of someone, you only needed to get them invited for dinner.

Have you heard? Your sister has been conscripted as a frontline defence against Imperialist missiles. She only has to lift her skirt and they'll head for home.

News flash on the radio. . . . Because of her untiring devotion to every man in the village, your fifteen-year-old daughter has been declared collectivized.

So sodden, so calumnious, was the return fire from the other side, lacking inventiveness as well as veracity, that it came as no surprise when our democratically chosen officers ordered us to respond in kind. Accordingly we replied, with an altogether heavier bore, with The Abject.

You clean your teeth in vulture's ordures and bathe in tomcat's urine to be appealing to your perfumed-in-jackal's-vomit whores.

Why do the rats flee your dugouts and the crabs scuttle from your bodies? Why do the moles dig deeper when you approach? Why do the crows fly higher? Questions you can't even smell the answer to.

Your officers eat dung hot from the camel, which you lackeys serve up to them on bended knee.

You converse through your anuses because your mouths are full of the irresistible contents of the officers' latrines.

And before they had a chance to collect their limited wits we hit them with Disease.

The haemorrhoids trail like vines from your desphinctered rectums.

The flatus from your ulcerated suppurating bellies makes even vultures flap off retching.

Rancid green slime oozes from your lice-infested, pocked, wizened genital organs. The next generation should be something to behold.

Cysts! Boils! Carbuncles! Warts! Herpes! Polyps! You have them and are them.

We could see we had done damage by the disarray in their encampment, especially in and near their mess tents, where our third salvo had been particularly lethal, but we had our own casualties to attend to and little time to celebrate the effectiveness of our fire-power. One young conscript, married only the day before his induction, had succumbed to a barbed shaft concerning his bride's purity, and was weeping inconsolably behind the kitchen tent. Even a veteran of this campaign, the much respected sergeant of our platoon had been unlucky enough to be touched by a stray remark concerning maggots in coffins, having received notification that very morning of the sudden death of his beloved brother.

This war of words is still war, dreadful and intemperate. Are the mutilations of the soul so less dreadful than those of the body? If their ruthless deployment of language could reduce our bravest to tears, could their artillery do worse? The military strategists for ever seek out new ways of conducting war. They maintain that for each person there is one particular combination of words which will wound so severely that the soul will shrivel and die. Their knowledge so far is rudimentary, and the insults we and they on the other side exchange are comparably crude. It is conceivable though that one day a phrase will come soughing across the Ussuri River to strike deep into the heart of one of the many who hear it, his nemesis, after which his body will go through the motions soullessly until its death, after which there will be nothing at all. Can even a nuclear shell do damage such as this? Is this arid infertile territory worth so much? These are the words of a doubter. The loudhailer lay at his feet. He picked it up and began to launch, together with his comrades, the first of the afternoon's attacks, Lack Of Intelligence.

What is your preferred drink? Vodka, if you can get it, and if not, ether, paraffin, gear oil, benzene. . . . No wonder your craniums contain nothing but a pus of dead braincells.
What is 1+2? How do you tie a bootlace? Which end of a gun does the bullet come out of? Questions from the passing out exam of the Soviet Military Academy.
Donkeys, sons of donkeys, your braying deceives only yourselves.
Cretins! Imbeciles! Your one hope is we shall die laughing at your shuffling, shambling, stumbling efforts to get your drooling mouths around insults a three-year-old would consider childish.
Followed by Fathers.

Is that your father we see, crawling out of the rubbish dump? But rats are too noble by far to have sired you.

You were conceived through sperm deposited on pictures of women he could never possess, which your mother scraped off the page into her womb.

He fled shrieking when a butterfly stared him in the face, and got given a medal for bravery.

And now he sits in his own excrement in the corner of his padded cell. He is wiser and cleaner than his son, however.

And Ancestry.

The souls of your ancestors, though barely human, howl with mirth at the degeneracy of their simian descendants. Only known case of evolution in reverse.

Your grandmother seduced her father who ravaged her daughter and made her your mother.

You had been told otherwise? Then they are liars as well as incestuous in your lineage.

Don't scratch, you'll disturb your incarnated ancestors feeding on your blood.

The sun burned down and the bare, rocky ground radiated it back, and we were in the middle between sun and earth. A kite perched motionless, notionless, in a blasted tree. The waters of the Ussuri thickened, stunned into immobility by the furnace. We gathered our energies for the last fusillade of the day, again in three volleys of four. The soldier sat with his back to the dried mud wall of the dugout, staring without seeing at the ants crawling over the floor with fragments of grain in their pincers. In his imagination there played a woman, getting old now, but then he was no longer young, whose face had always defied his complete understanding and always incited his longing to return to her. And what a cook! The thought of egg-enriched noodles, spicy with eels and the legs of the frogs that swarm in the irrigation ditches, accompanied by pickled cabbage, brought moisture to his parched mouth. Why were we at war with our fellow socialists? In a parallel universe, with as awful weather, our conflict is being waged with explosives and hot metal, bodies lying squandered in their thousands on the carmine-stained ground. Despite misgivings about damage to soul, our way with words is probably preferable. Insults are only lethal when delivered by special person, something the militarists forget. From slobs like them across the great water, not much harm forthcoming. He sighed, picked up the loudhailer. The evening bombardment would begin with Sexuality.

Cluck! cluck! Your members are encrusted with the menstrual blood of chickens. Oink! oink! Your officers get to goose geese.

Why do you raid the cemetery for your women? Is it because living they make too many demands on you?

Is it children we see at their ablutions once a month? Can that tuft of hair conceal a male member? A few more years, comrades, and your gonads will drop.

The Russian military salute? Bending over with trousers down.

Then Damnation.

If heaven were a latrine and hell a palace, you would have no trouble achieving Enlightenment.

Your afterlives will be even more squalid than your present existence, with only yourself for company.

Preferred habitat of Russian soul? Gobs of sputum underfoot.

Your soul is a worm tied in a knot. No hands. No helper.

And finally, The Body Of The Mother.

Your mother's joy is to embrace the Chinese army, including the latrine cleaners.

Why did she reject you at the breast? Could it be she preferred the honeyed tongue of a Chinese soldier?

She risks her life to swim the Ussuri River? To get away from you or to come to us? Are they so different?

When she saw you emerging from between her legs she laughed out loud. Hasn't stopped since. What a joke!

And so, as our shadows stretched eastward, we came to the end of it, our abuse and theirs, across the silent waters between us. Over the thirty-nine steppes we had expressed our forty insults. A day's battle, a necessary task, that few had taken pleasure in, while many had suffered pain. Their words, though not refined, have a certain brutal power it is hard to ignore. It is said that there are those whose souls are so close to heaven that words cannot harm them, for they entertain no illusions and nurture no desires. The soldier who

111

imagined the woman from far away Sichuan was not among them. Not only their abuse but our own had diminished him, shaming him as he uttered it. He was unworthy to be the son of the mother he loved. After ablution there must be penance, but before either there was the preparation of vegetables to be done. He laid down the loudhailer and took out his knife, testing the blade against his thumb. Wild fennel must be sliced translucently thin to be palatable. In Sichuan his mother was writing a letter to her granddaughter, his niece, telling her of the success they had had this year in raising chickens, ducks too, and enquiring of favourite relative why her mother, her daughter, his sister was so tardy in writing. She pressed the completed letter briefly to her lips and put it in the envelope that would transport it to another faraway place, our city where Joyce, so pleased to hear from her gran, and I would read it at breakfast over our flakes of maize and ox's milk.

Eleven

The eponymous cur, prime recipient of La Jefe's love, roamed freely through the onyx and marble, teak and sandalwood salons of the Chihuahua Club, sidling up to patrons who would pause in their pursuits and give it a pat to encourage it to plague someone else. All, within the bounds of decorum, might be permitted to members, but shame on any who didn't give Puch, known out of La Jefe's earshot as Puke, a moment of her time. Its pink, hairless, constantly trembling body, with veined translucent ears, bore the scars of many a battle with its great enemy Pique, the peke belonging to the General, who was in turn La Jefe's great rival for the patronage of the women of means of our city. They would meet, the four of them, for luncheon alternate Sundays at one or other of their establishments, the Chihuahua Club and Au-Delà du Principe de Plaisir, where the dogs would snarl under the table and the two entrepreneurs would beam above it. The thoughts of Puch and Pique remain theirs alone, but that of their owners were well-documented in the gloss their clients were handed on arrival, summed up by La Jefe's slogan 'Live Copiously' and the General's 'Chaos Is Truth'. Surprisingly the General's corporeal plentitude was as notable as La Jefe's lack of it, as if each waxed or waned on the philosophy of the other. They were content to let their dogs express their differences, while they themselves savoured each other's considerable company.

In order of priority, three things mattered to La Jefe: Puch, the management of the Chihuahua Club, and her luncheons with the General. So when Puch went missing these latter could not but be affected. Following searches of the porphyry and agate, walnut and ebony halls of the Chihuahua Club, then its immediate environs, then the length and breadth of our city, La Jefe offered a million peso reward, which generated a series of lookalikes hauled out of the pound by indigents looking for easy money, but no Puch. From the isolation of her private penthouse suite, she thanked the General for the gross of white roses and come-back-soon card from

Pique and regretted that all engagements, including even their fortnightly tête-à-tête, were cancelled until further notice. Then, as the days turned into weeks, the signs barely perceptible at first, of the withdrawal of La Jefe's guiding managerial hand became evident to the club's clientèle.

In the basement, the various combinations of hot and cold, wet and dry, became unreliable, with gusts of chill air blasting the sauna, and sudden puffs of scalding steam through the perforated floor of the cooling-off room, and the temperature of the Turkish bath dropping to the point where it began to rain on its users. At the poolside the service so deteriorated that members were making bets as to which ways their orders would be incorrectly filled. Triple decker sandwiches would become double deckers, Pimms No 1 would taste suspiciously like No 2, and Perrier would be served up flat as Malvern water. The crèche, up till then a model of infant care, was afflicted by an outbreak of diarrhoea that no amount of disinfecting was able to eradicate. In the sports section, mishaps became frequent, both minor like spongy tennis rackets and biased squash balls, and major, like the snapping of one of the parallel bars in the gym, which landed the gymnast in hospital. In the beauty salon members found that the facials were bringing them out in lobster-red welts, depilatory wax treatments seemed to be conducted with casual brutality and the manicures left scagged nails and sore quicks. The restaurants, both minceur and gourmand, whose reputations had fully justified their rosettes, were the subject of continuous and appalled discussion as dish after dish was returned to the kitchens. Collapsed soufflées, separated Hollandaise, underdone pork, overdone beef, broccoli indistinguishable from school cabbage, tinned asparagus, synthetic cream and imported strawberries became commonplace, while the wines acquired vices taken from the pages of the Marquis de Sade. Even the upper floors, where decorous quietude was an axiom, suffered their own appropriate forms of degradation. In the bridge room players found coffee stains on the green cloth of their tables, cards missing from the pack and lead missing from the propelling pencils provided with the score sheets. The Wall Street Journal began to appear a vital day late in the reading room, and fashion magazines arrived with pages cut out, as if the Chihuahua

Club were some dentist's waiting room dependent on cast-offs. Even the Astarte Temple, where those so inclined could achieve the transfiguring experience of the higher spiritual planes, was not immune from gremlins, as became evident when the incense-burner emitted a foul smell reminiscent of fish-bone manure and the hi-fi system inexplicably blared forth the Sex Pistols in place of Ravi Shankar. Worst of all, disputes among members erupted without cause and over the most trivial matters, including, unprecedently, men. One member went so far as to publicly denounce another as the efficient cause of her husband's newly acquired venereal complaint, and followed up the accusation with a bombardment of éclairs seized from the pâtisserie's display. In short, without the chihuahua, the Chihuahua was not the Chihuahua.

Unsubstantiated rumours as to Puch's fate spread through the chalcedony and jasper, box and rosewood chambers of the club. Some detected the hand of the General in the disappearance, with variations according to whether Pique had slaughtered its enemy, requiring an immediate cover-up, or whether the General herself had abducted Puch in order to gain a competitive edge over her thus demoralized rival. The most scurrilous variant on this theme referred to a recent infamous occurrence at Au-Delà when the roast and lacquered corpse of a pet dog had been served up to its distraught owners, middle-aged American tourists who spoke not a word of the French that the General insisted should be the only language in which orders would be accepted, who had imagined that by pointing to their mouths, then at their dog, that it, not they, would be fed. The rumour-mongers proposed that the General had switched Puch for their pooch, so providing a brilliant alibi. Others expected that a ransom demand would soon be forthcoming, though they were split on whether it would come from the Triads or the RSPCA. Another line of speculation was that Puch had simultaneously developed amnesia and a sudden growth of body hair and was therefore wandering through our city lost and unrecognized. One school of thought was inclined to see a truly Machiavellian plot originating with none other than La Jefe herself, who was deemed to have slaughtered her dog in order to provide an excuse to run the club down so she could secretly acquire the forty-nine percent of shares not already in her hands at knockdown prices. Since the only known adherents to this calumnious theory were the two grand-daughters of La Jefe and the General respectively, with whom their relations were not cordial, it was largely discounted.

Then, one Tuesday morning in late May, an orderly about to polish the mother-of-pearl and tortoiseshell, cherry and satinwood hallway of the Chihuahua Club saw what caused him to scatter his brooms and flee to the cleaners' mess, from where the dreadful intelligence was passed up and through the administrative hierarchy eventually to reach La Jefe's amanuensis, a tall, spare Scotswoman with a liking for Höl-derlin but little else, who after due consideration decided that nothing of substance could be gained by procrastination. This brave lady thus had the unenviable task of relaying to her employer first the good news that Puch had returned, second the bad that Puch was frozen into immobility, like a single frame out of an action movie, by the taxiderimist's art. Whether out of loyalty or because of an unwillingness to repeat the trauma of the revelation, Miss McGibbon could never be persuaded to say what La Jefe's first word had been, but her subsequent were recorded through the quick thinking of a waiter with a portable Sony cassette recorder which he switched on as she came to the stairhead, terrible in an orchidaceous yellow dressing gown.

Who killed poor Puch?

To the perpetrator of the deed, no mercy.

Bring forth the instruments of torture, that all may gaze on them.

Such love as Puch's is perfect.

The Chihuahua Club is to be a mausoleum from this day hence.

A sacrifice must be made; prepare libations and sharpen knives; Pique shall also die.

Since no one was inclined to gainsay La Jefe in her hour of wrath, the General, who liked to sleep late in her sun-drenched apartment on one of the avenues radiating like a star from our city's triumphal arch, was hastily summoned to attend to her friend. It was inconceivable, natually, that La Jefe's demand for Pique's blood would be met, but more than blood-red roses were called for now. So the General woke Pique, who also liked to sleep late, and bundled it into the limousine waiting outside, engine purring. When they arrived at the opal and alabaster, bamboo and palisander entrance hall of the Chihuahua Club, La Jefe was poised next to her freeze-frame pet, the sacrificial knife raised in isomorphic complementarity to its cutely extended forepaw. On spotting its old enemy and suspecting an imminent coup de théâtre from either or both the General or La Jefe, Pique promptly converted its endemic snuffling into a despairing ear-splitting howl.

Whereupon there occurred what is told to each new member as she is conducted through the clam-shell and lapis lazuli, cedar and jacaranda rooms of the Chihuahua Club and will be retold as she sweats in the sauna, or eats sachertort in the pâtisserie, or reads Pravda in the library, or plays piquet in the games room, a tale of such incredibility that incredulity is the first response, yielding to acceptance only through its interminable repetition. As the screeching, scratching, puk-ing, peeing peke Pique was carried by the General towards La Jefe, over the left glass eye of the stuffed chihuahua an eyelid fluttered. Puch, by some unseen hand at an undetected radio transmitter sited deep beneath the hills to the east of our city, had been activated. In quick succession, the tail rose, the mouth opened, and the body began its characteristic unstoppable trembling. Puch, more properly 'Puch', a simulacrum of Puch, had been resurrected and, what is more, sensing by means of photo-electric cells and identifying with the 256K digital memory its ancient enemy, flew at Pique's throat. As Puch and Pique renewed their struggle for supre-macy on the rock crystal and obsidian, tulip and maple floor of the Chihuahua Club, La Jefe and the General, reprieved from symbolic necessity, embraced. Whatever 'Puch's' ontological status, it was effectively indistinguishable from the original, as shown by the red oozing from a nasty bite

Pique had succeeded in inflicting on its hind leg. Joyfully, the dogs' owners pulled their pets apart and there began, on La Jefe's decree, a celebration which for a year and a day would make of the jade and mother-of-pearl, thuya and huang hua-li wood inner spaces of the Chihuahua Club something not far short of paradise.

Twelve

Gropius the exile stands beneath an arch of the line connecting our city's two railway termini. He turns up the collar of his trenchcoat against the rain sleeting in on him. A train rumbles overhead. On the wall behind him is sprayed in aerosol:

>After years of continence he threw himself into a sea of six women. £.

Beneath it is scrawled in blood:

>Some chance. Frank.

He fingers the three coins with holes through the middle that he keeps for consulting the I Ching, authorship attributed to King Wên, godfather of the Chou dynasty. All they know of Gropius' mind derives from the chain of signs he acts upon in answer to the questions he constantly puts to the oracle. Each question can receive 2^{12} answers, because any of the six lines in sixty-four hexagrams can change to the opposite, yin to yang, yang to yin. Then there are the interpretations, infinitely many, though more than that are barred. The Book tells where you're at and where you're about to be at. Having committed the text and its many commentaries to memory, Gropius uses it to chart a path through the maze of women in his life, at any one time always six in number.

He gets Po, Splitting Apart. Po for Polly. Polly for whom he is presumed to be splitting apart for want of her soul, even while she parts her legs for him and anyone else with twenty pounds to spend. Here's the hexagram:

The Judgement is not favourable. It advises:

>*It does not further one to go anywhere.*

But Gropius is getting cold and wet, too much yin not enough yang, underneath the arch. A skein of geese whistle overhead to the reservoir where they'll pass the night. Pulling

119

his collar up higher he crosses the greasy street to a phone booth, inserts a dime, dials a number. A car accelerates away from the light in a snarl of exhaust, a squeal of tyres. Gropius has had enough. The kopek drops.

Clemency picks up the phone. Gropius' voice says, 'Gropius'. Clemency says, 'You can come round if you want to.' She senses something has changed, not yet knowing it's a line in the fifth place, which means:

> *A shoal of fishes.*
> *Favour comes through the court of ladies.*
> *Everything acts to further.*

Polly she knows about, having heard his anguished, hallowed castigations, having followed the geography of her body, every blemish, every perfection recounted with loving attention to detail. Three days, three years, she forgets how long Gropius has been desperate for his impossible girl. With him Clemency has touched, tasted, sensed the texture of her skin, breathed in the oils of her hair, even as she herself has been astride him in the kitchen, skirt up, no knickers, with Gerald in the living room watching sport on television. They've always had time for her to slip up, off, and on to the adjacent chair whenever Gerald's come through for a refill, without a break in the conversation. Aroused more by his story-telling than she is troubled by jealousy, she understands that whatever makes Gropius tick he has a way with women. She appreciates his attentions not only to her own nipples which are hard beneath her blouse as she puts the phone down and checks the finishing time of the big match but to the sacred zones of others, that he's hinted differ from woman to woman. Polly's, she suspects, might be her ear, glittering with rings, multiply pierced up to and beyond the cartilage, into which one tender night Gropius is reputed to have whispered after handing over his cash that he would die in order to give her a baby, causing Clemency to come in an unanticipated babble of joy and Gerald to call through to keep the noise down, it was a black ball game. Polly had chuckled and said maybe, Gropius mumbled into Clemency's vulva. A part of her pleasure comes from the wish that Polly be her daughter, the child of a union between her and Gropius, or even her and Gropius's father whoever he might be, and that she half-knowingly permit the incest to take place, perhaps in the bedroom above the kitchen, while she does the ironing beneath. At other times she supposes that Polly denies herself completely to Gropius, while regaling him with her exploits with the Real Man Chester football team, which Gerald supports, especially the six foot six black keeper, a magician on the box. It's not altogether an unlikely hypothesis, for each story he tells differs slightly from its predecessor, as if the truth were constantly rejigged to allow for shifts in present circumstances. Thus constituted are her relations with the other women he loves and/or who love him, not just Polly but four more. In the process he as tale-bearer fades, until he is no more than a messenger bearing messages he cannot read among the six women, each of whom has her own version of the other five and her own relation to the rest. Clemency's liaison with Gropius the wanderer has lasted longer than most. During it the balance of power/love has shifted decisively at least twice. Before the last she consoled herself with the thought that where equality is impossible, better to love than be loved. Since Polly, though, he's became newly devoted to her and as altogether athletic as the shot putters she can hear grunting on the channel Gerald's switched to. A rejuvenated Gropius, almost to the stage of infancy, is what she's enjoying, and she wonders whether Pru Fell, the other mother he says he loves, takes similar pleasures, say shampooing his hair while he shuts his little eyes tight against the lather. She'd wash him, standing barebummed and dripping, in the kitchen sink if she could think of a way to pass it off as unremarkable if Gerald came through. And somehow in the interim she does. So Gropius stands contemplating – like, like, like a broken-down Turkic patriarch trailing packmules, ducks, children, being washed for his sins by the woman in the first place as the setting sun turns the windswept rye-grass of the steppe into a shimmering ocean of gold.

The hexagram generated by the changing line is Kuan,

觀

Contemplation. The Judgement reads:

> *The ablution has been made,*
> *But not yet the offering.*
> *Full of trust they look up to him.*

Clemency smiles and rinses Gropius' thighs as the pok pok pok of tennis drifts down the hallway.

Elsewhere in the city the object of the erotic dialogue that is about to ensue between Gropius and Clemency is about to conduct a lucrative transaction with a star tennis player here for the Northern Tournament.

The Tao is everywhere and embraces everyone.

Thirteen

The doorbell interrupted my Mex-and-Booris-induced sleep, complete with balalaika dreams. They'd departed before dawn, after we'd exchanged addresses, and by my watch it was now midday. This must be the Professor come to debrief me. But it wasn't. Nothing's that simple.

It was the thin man, distinctly the worse for wear, with a yellow smear of egg on the lilac of his tie, swaying in the doorway with a large tattered package in his arms. As he stumbled a pace forward, I put my arm around his shoulders to steady him. Shockingly, my hand encountered a knife sticking out from his back. Slowly he sank to his knees, then sprawled full-length, the package rolling heavily across the floor to finish up against the far wall. Without my knowing it my fingers must have closed around the haft of the knife as he fell, for I was standing over him, brandishing it, for all the world as if I was the killer. But worse was to come. The package had banged into and switched back on the wall plug connected to I-LID's video camera, which I'd switched off with proper reticence before the celebrations of the night before. The On light was lit, the camera was pointing in my direction, and I was caught for ever in the act on magnetic no-wipe tape. Talk about being framed. I was at their mercy, whoever they were.

Adolphus, unfazed by my predicament, was sniffing around the package. To satisfy his curiosity, or maybe I had an idea what was going to be in it, I cut the string with the knife and unwrapped the layers of newspaper. My hunch was right.

The Maltese falcon, pride of the knights of St John, in its disguise of black enamel, stood before me. Somehow the wily Russian general in Istambul who'd outwitted Greenstreet and company every Christmas on TV for as long as I could recall had managed to land it on me. The big question was now, was it a f-f-fake or the real thing? A c-c-copy or the original? Putting the knife to a third use, I tentatively scored the enamel. The paint peeled away along the groove to reveal a gleam of gold beneath. I took a deep breath, if only to quell the stammer I'm susceptible to when excited. I was one rich sister. The falcon had been worth a million back in '41 when Spade worked for twenty-five dollars a day and bread was a penny a loaf. One thing was, not everyone was going to be as happy as me I'd become the possessor of twenty megabucks worth of macguffin. There was also the little matter of the corpse figured on the I-LID carpet. The time had come, I concluded, to make myself scarce.

I scooped the falcon up under one arm, Adolphus under the other, and headed out the flat and down the stairwell past graffiti advising me the dead were right. As one of the living left I felt distinctly in the dark. I came out into the pale wintry sunshine, another cruel April, and blinked twice, once for the light, once for the police car blocking my passage. 'Get in, MacGnash', the sergeant ordered, bundling me into the back seat next to a lieutenant I knew from somewhere else, because this was a police-free zone except for search-and-destroy raids. I prepared myself for a friendly chat in the soundproof cells of the station. But they sped west along the highway out of the city. Neither of them would be drawn as to our destination, so I sat back and admired the scenery, derelict factories for the most part, with nature scrubbily reasserting itself among them. We came to a small airfield, where they pulled to a halt in front of a low building. Standing there, consulting her watch, was the Professor. The cop beside me leant over, copping a feel of my thigh as he did so, and opened the car door. With my cargo of creatures animate and inanimate still clutched securely, I got out.

'I was beginning to wonder if anything unfortunate had befallen you. It is a great relief to find you alive and well.'

'More than some people, Professor.'

She glanced at me sharply as we hurried north by Northwest Airlines check-in counter and out on to the apron. 'Has there been. . . ?'

'Too right. Another accident. And it looks like I'm the fall guy.' Briefly I outlined the circumstances of the arrival of the falcon, but not my subsequent discovery of its worth.

'Dreadful, dreadful.'

'Two down, one to go,' I said, not feeling anything like so

callous as I sounded, just sensitive to the necessities of the plot.

'It makes it all the more imperative that we act swiftly. Are you aware of the significance of what you are carrying?'

'Augustus? He's just a dumb cat.'

'I was referring', said the Professor, with just the degree of emphasis to warn me flippancy was *not* appreciated, 'to what you carry under your other arm.'

'It's just a blackbird. Isn't it?'

'Let us simply say for the moment that it bears meaning.'

'That's all right by me,' I said, thinking only of its value. So far as I was concerned it meant making movies on the grand scale. I'll sell my soul for art.

We were approaching a cropdusting plane and the rest of our conversation was drowned by the roar of its single engine. But what I'd heard already was enough to convince me of the need to board it, along with my cat and trophy.

Julia Jane – now we were saying goodbye I felt I could call her that – helped me up behind the pilot who bore an uncanny resemblance to Cary Grant. Inside the cockpit I settled myself on a wooden crate of chickens, clucking. Adolphus inserted a paw between the slats until a sharp peck from a rooster made him reconsider his tactics. Julia Jane smiled up at me encouragingly and mouthed, 'Need to simulate flight. Put them off the trail. Think you're fleeing to the East. Don't forget to pull the ripcord.'

I shouted back down, 'Then what?'

'Events will unfold. Don't worry.'

The flimsy plane was vibrating enough to blur my vision, like the sprocket holes in a movie had come adrift. Julia Jane kicked away the chocks with her alligator-skin shoes. Then, after an eternity of bumping down the runway, we were airborne, just in time to clear a petrol tanker on the long straight road across the flatlands beyond the airstrip. The plane banked steeply and I could see Julia Jane waving, a microscopic dot in the silver halide panorama below. Before long we passed over our city and were approaching the hills to the east of it. A train, one I could have been on heading in comfort to Stamboul and a jubilant Black Sea dip with Mex and Booris, pulled clear of the suburbs and disappeared into a tunnel. The pilot turned and indicated I should put on the parachute. I hoped Julia Jane had taken the weight of the black bird and my ginger puss into account in making her calculations. The pilot, such a nice face, pointed at his watch. One minute. Adolphus seemed intent on joining the chickens in their crate. But he was coming with me, and so was the falcon. With them once again under each arm, I prepared to make my jump, a matter of tilting off backwards over the side of the rear cockpit. The pilot raised, then lowered his hand. Bye Cary, back I went, arse over tit, into the wild peachy pink yonder.

Free fall was wonderful, like I'd been born to it. I could have stood it for ever, the wind in my hair, the sun on my back. But time was not on my side.

Julia Jane had said to count down from six, slowly, then to pull the yellow tag. At three I began to think about it, at two I made a move and at one I yelled blue murder – with a cat under one arm and the whatsit under the other, there was no way I could reach it. It was either love or money, one of them had to go. Put it down to my being left-handed, but I let the money fall, to accelerate into millstone grit at Mach whatever. I pulled my tag, not a hundred metres too soon, a sudden jolt, then drifting in a tranquil stillness, broken only by the songs of skylarks, the distant drone of the plane and the grateful miaows of my cat.

We landed in a gully overhung by rowan, terraced strata down which a beck rushed. I felt quite lightheaded, almost lyrical. Adolphus too, from the way he leapt from rock to rock. There are times when it's all right. What did I care about the money. Upstream, on a broad flat rock, lay the fragments of the falcon, fool's gold and shards of coloured glass. In the centre of the shattered dream, another Poisson distribution, there lay, I saw as I stooped to investigate, a familiar curl of microfilm, fluttering in the breeze like a severed butterfly's wing. I picked it up and my mood changed.

I'd told Mex and Booris there'd been three. Maybe I'd been telling more than I knew. Maybe I knew more than I knew. Whichever, here was the second, a blueprint if ever there was one, with the contours of the hills I was in clearly defined, along with a spot marked X just up the hillside. I had to admire Julia Jane's means even if I couldn't comprehend her ends. She evidently had planned all this, the phoney falcon, the precise landing place, my double armful, my noble sacrifice, in order that I should be the bearer of a message that couldn't have been revealed even under torture. But this was as far as I was going. So far and no further. I stood on the lip of the pot, a black hole fringed by coarse grass, and felt a chill miasma seeping from it. I'm okay on heights, cats don't give me allergies, and I just adore spiders. But put me in a cramped space, in the dark, and I'm a gibbering wreck. They could carry on without me. Sometimes a woman's just got to say no.

The first bullet whined past my head and kicked up a clod of earth behind me. A figure on horseback was outlined against the sky on the top of the bluff on the far side of the gully. The figure had a rifle. The rifle was pointing my way.

I began to run and heard the crack of a second shot, followed by a yowl of pain. I stopped and turned. Adolphus was somersaulting through the air in a slow arc. The bastard had got my cat.

I looked for cover. There was only the rowan tree back down by the stream. It was a long way off. I'd never make it. There was just place left to hide, the hole in the hillside I swore I'd never be found dead in. My legs were pumping, my heart pounding. I was almost there. I heard the third shot fractionally after I felt the slug slam into my ribs like a car door crunching a finger. I heard myself cough. A productive cough. I stumbled back a pace. My foot didn't touch ground. The figure on the hillside was fringed with red. I could now see it was a woman. She seemed to be wearing a red swimsuit, and the gun she was carrying looked ominously like a scythe. I was still falling, twice in an afternoon, except this time it wasn't through clear blue mountain air, it was down a shaft of blackness, into a well of roaring silence. Mother of mercy, was this the end of Fur Q Films?

THIRD THIRD

No, it wasn't. But I might have been better off if it had been. I came to in a room built to withstand an infinitude of pain, having presumably been brought there unconscious after my fall. The walls were pitted grey, splodged with streaks of rusty brown. On the metal door, in yellow aerosol paint, was scrawled, YOU'RE ALREADY DEAD. In the corner was a heavy duty battery, attacked to jump leads, that I didn't like the look of. Next to it lay the corpse of a chihuahua. My wrists and ankles were wired tight to an iron chair bolted to the floor. I could smell vomit, possibly my own. I wasn't alone for long. The door swung wide and in came three people. I say people. I say I. I ran my tongue over parched lips and croaked. 'I guess I was played for a sucker.'

'There's one born every minute,' said the General. 'You expected an even break?'

'You're all washed up, MacTrash,' said the colonel. 'Your future's all used up.'

I didn't care they were plundering movies I held dear. I wasn't even listening to what they said. What had grabbed my attention was who they'd brought with them. She was about my age, a little older, a little fatter. In her right hand she was holding an axe. It wasn't that though that brought a scream bubbling up out of my lungs and had me wishing the lady on horseback had made a better job of it. It was the knowledge I'd moved into another genre. Film noir was my neck of the woods, spy stuff I could just about cope with, but the fantastic was unknown territory. I knew the third person well enough. She was me.

'Horace does tend to exaggerate,' the General said, as my scream died away in the soundproofed fortress of the torture chamber, 'all we want is for you to co-operate.'

'Just tell me how.'

'Show her the instruments, honey.'

At his spouse's instruction the colonel nodded at my double, who swung the axehead hissing past my bound torso.

'Can't you see who I am, you idiot?' I snarled at her, in a sudden access of powerless rage. 'You're torturing yourself.'

The General said sympathetically, 'It's no good arguing with her. She's fully programmed to do exactly what we want. A perfect simulacrum. You'd never tell her from the original. Synthesized organs, printed circuitry, solid state brain. The ultimate commodity.'

The colonel put in, 'Or if that's too tough for you, you could think of her as a monster from the id.'

I hated science fiction. I searched for an epithet. 'Plagiarist!' Then, weakly, 'I'll id you.'

Talk about feeding him lines. Smugly, he came back 'I-LID's everywhere.'

'What is this', I groaned, 'a comedy?'

'Not for long, sister,' said the colonel, and turned to my treacherous mirror image. 'Hit her.'

My precarious universe exploded into a firmament of pain. I heard a rib crack as the axehead thudded into my side.

'Next time it'll be the sharp end,' the colonel informed me.

'We want a name,' the General said.

Under the right circumstances, people'll do anything, say anything. I said, 'Anna.'

The colonel nodded at my double. 'Finish her off.'

This time it was the sharp end.

The axehead circled once and severed my head from my torso.

The axehead circled once and severed her head from her torso.

'Cut her loose,' the colonel commanded me.

With a few taps of the axe the bonds parted, and the headless body slumped to the floor a way away from the bodiless head that had rolled into the corner to finish up alongside the dead chihuahua. In sympathy I rubbed the welt on my skin, tentatively probed beneath my left breast. The T-shirt under my denim jacket was sticking to my flesh. It seemed like I was a perfect copy, down to the last detail, complete with my original's memory. I remember I'd been shot, out there on the hillside. The bullet had hit me over my heart, I'd tasted blood. I reached inside my jacket. The flesh there seemed intact, if badly bruised. It was another mystery. Not even I-LID's credit card could have deflected a bullet, and besides, that was in the back pocket of my jeans. Solving it was going to have to wait. It seemed like they were in a

132

hurry. They led me along along neon-lit corridors, the colonel opening gas-proof, radiation-proof, virus-proof firedoors at each intersection by feeding a code number into their digital locks. For all her bulk the General moved swiftly. We entered a lift, the doors closed, we waited, the doors opened, and we stepped out.

I gasped. As far as the eye could see there were uniformed technical personnel seated at computer consoles, while down the aisles between them patrolled surveillance officers. Overhead a series of vast video displays revealed all I'd never wanted to know about the Soviet Union and its global influence. No conscript in Murmansk was going to blow his nose without it being detected, projected and incorporated into simulated battle scenarios. On one screen close by I could see the muddy waters of the Ussuri River meandering through the disputed border territory in the heartland of Asia, while adjacent speakers relayed the invective flying from one side to the other. I'd have lingered to listen, nothing like a good slanging match, but the General hurried on as ranking officers snapped to attention in her wake. I wondered if they'd have been so deferential if they'd known about her allegiance to the force de frappe, targetted no doubt to reassert Franco-colonial dominion once the Soviets and the Anglos had fought each other to a standstill around the globe. Eventually, after trekking for what seemed like hours through the ranks of this electronic army, we came to the far side of the command bunker, where there was a door marked Off Limits To Unauthorized Personnel. I assumed that meant me. I was wrong, yet again.

'Sorry, Horace, you don't have the clearance,' said the General to her husband. To me, 'We can make an exception for you, honey.'

Though small recompense for what I'd gone through at his hands, it still felt good to say, 'Bye Y', over my shoulder as I followed the General through the door, 'One place fritz doesn't get in, know what I mean?' The General I'd get even with some other time.

My vengeance plans were cut short by the next encounter. I might have known it. The Professor, seated at a computer console, intensely frowning, Gucci shoes tapping the floor in a vibrato of nerves. At our entry she turned and worriedly asked, 'She talked?'

'With a little persuasion.'

The Professor, bless her, shook her head in distress, saying, 'I do deplore these methods. I hope you haven't been too severely discomforted, my dear.'

'Hell, no. Just a couple of scratches.'

'Most regrettable, none the less. You are in the unfortunate position of being the bearer of a message whose existence you did not even suspect and whose contents are unknown to you, not incomparable to that of the Greek messenger-slaves whose shaven heads were tattooed while they slept to be read by others when they had reached their destination.'

'The third blueprint?'

'Even we do not know that. We only anticipate. That was why it was essential to obtain the access key from you.'

The General said, 'It's Anna. Same as my impossible granddaughter.'

'A coincidence, I am sure. Also a palindrome.'

'No coincidence. My granddaughter's too,' said a gravelly voice, as into the cathode-ray light there stepped a formidable old woman, whose granitic face was etched with lines of power. I instantly judged her a match for the General.

'I don't think you've met,' said the Professor, ever ready with the introductions. 'La Jefe.'

'I don't think I have,' I said, as this person took my hand in a vicelike grip and held my eyes in one similar. 'I'm sure I'd have remembered.'

'We have had our differences, la Générale and I, but in our mutual interest to ensure stability, we have agreed to act in concert. Between us we control the city. But our grand-daughters are running amok, spreading rumour and subversion, threatening to disrupt our global partition. They've got into the Showdown programme. That means the game's no longer zero sum. We could both be the losers.'

'Anna!' the General said. 'Yours, Conchita, and mine. The ungrateful little bitches. We should have guessed.'

'Damn right. And left me to making movies.'

'Shuddup. Or we mince you up and feed you to the goldfish.'

La Jefe was no wishy-washy liberal, I noted.

Nor, for that matter, was the General. 'Get on with it,

Professor. Use your brains. That's what we're both paying you for. Hook it out.'

While we'd been chatting the Professor however had been busy at her console, feeding in questions as fast as the computer could flash them back. Now she said, 'It's not going to be easy. ANNA's linked into configurations which seemed to extend throughout the whole system. The effects of premature isolation of any one of them would be incalculable. It could result in total breakdown.'

'You designed Showdown, Professor, you should be able to undesign it.'

'It may not be possible.'

'Everything's possible.'

The incipient philosophical debate between the Professor's critical realism and the General's power of positive thinking was cut short by La Jefe banging her fist on top of the console. 'If you can't get ANNA out, there's only one thing to do. Use it. Activate it.'

The effect of the suggestion on both her companions was dramatic. Julia Jane, gastrotopologist, double if not triple agent, advanced driver, fluttered a hand up to her throat and murmured faintly, 'I, for one, could not take the responsibility.'

And petite Sophie, a hundred kilos in weight, a hundred megabucks in the Shanghai and Suburban, with I-LID in her pay and staff officers cringing before her, could only pass the buck and say, 'I do not have the authority. But you, Conchita, are you prepared to enact your suggestion?'

At the challenge, Conchita, Godmother of our city's co-domain, owner and Hon. Sec. of the Chihuahua Club, looked uncomfortable. 'Assuredly. But my hands are tied. The management committee, you understand. The price one pays of running a democratic organization.'

'So we're back where we started. Fishing.'

'Not quite, Sophie. We three may be restricted, but not so her.'

Her, I realized as their three looks converged in an indisputable triangulation, was me. Being a simulacrum didn't make me feel any less me either. I blinked. They were still there, unblinking, thinking the unthinkable, and I knew what that was. It was me that was figured as the one to press the

Showdown button. I'd come up with ANNA, out of nowhere, and it was me who was destined to go down with her, into the unknown, taking the world with me, or not, as the case might be, while the lady in the red swimsuit sharpened her scythe, chuckling.

What the hell.

'Okay, just show me where to put my finger.'

They did, after hours of organizing entry protocols, clearing channels through the military-industrial hierarchy, checking with the seismologists about tectonic activity along the San Andreas fault (they got it wrong), alerting the Politburo, warning the White House, etc etc, while I idled away the time watching Dr Strangelove on the Off Limits recreational video. Eventually it was all taken care of.

The Professor said, 'We shall leave you now. The screen will indicate the countdown, beginning at five to midnight. On the stroke of twelve, you push this. The rest will depend on ANNA. I hope we'll meet again. Don't know where. Don't know when. Some happy day.'

I could tell the Professor was all choked up, her syntax was unrecognizable. There was nothing more to be said. The General and La Jefe had already departed arm in arm, arguing vociferously, along with everyone else. In a sudden surge of emotion I clasped Julia Jane to me and silently whispered 'Bye, grannie'. Then she was gone and I was alone. The hour was approaching. I wondered where Amadeus was, whether he was still alive. It was coming up to midnight. I crossed my fingers, just for luck. And pressed the button.

Two

The personal is professional, as the current adage so compellingly puts it. Never one to step out of line, I have decided to conclude my hagiography, though protesting at its brevity, one thirteenth really isn't much of a share, by concentrating on Mac★★ash's contribution to our city's film culture. What went on before I was around is impossible to say, with opaque cans thwarting my desire to project their transparencies through the apparatus she but not I can manage. Instead it's a matter of recollecting those I was in on the making of, when I would saunter through the prefilmic real, cast an eye through the viewfinder, insinuate myself into the editing room, rub up against the final print, and if the odd hair detached itself to catch in the gate of the projector and irritate spectators with its extra-diegetic flicker, what small price to pay for authenticity.

Caff was where I came in, and in a sorry state, for it was during the shooting of this she adopted me. Mac★★ash then was committed to a politics of 'less is more', and following such prescriptions the action consisted of a cycle of near-identical transactions at a cash register in a motorway café, thirty-five minutes of shots of food on trays, hands ringing up the amount, money handed over, face of woman on the till, ended but not closed by the grant running out. I loved it, having scoffed the choicest leftovers from its representations.

Tireless self-criticism, coupled with the faint praise of her co-workers, led on to the next stage in Mac★★ash's aesthetic maturation. She conceded that spectators would find stories even where none were intended, since spectating itself presumed the fatal lack all narrative attempts to fill. Better then to provide ample evidence of the lack in abundant story-telling under the rubric 'More is more'. Costa originated with a scurrilous account by two girls we picked up on the motorway of their just-completed Spanish holiday, which so inspired Mac★★ash that she asked them to play themselves in the film she'd make from it. They, delighted, acted out their rewritten-as-a-Restoration-drama history of passion, treachery, rapine, assassination and mayhem against the backcloth, painted by our camerawoman, of Torremolinos in July. The film won a prize at San Sebastian, where I was not allowed to go for our national paranoia I'd come back rabid.

Over-elated by success my dear mistress fell prey to the delusion she'd established her cinematic practice as impeccable. The rubbishing of Pork, makes, therefore, a cautionary tale, which I shall tell so that others can avoid her errors. 'Too much' is far from necessarily, as she'd fondly proposed, 'even more'. Conceived as a parody that would expostulate the lineaments of pornography for reasoned critique, it was dogged, how apt some words are, by misfortune from the outset.

The film's female lead was a fine young saddleback sow called Girt borrowed from an urban collective farm, her co-stars a pair of lissome studs known as Jack and Jock hired from the We'll Call You casting agency. The two Js blanched somewhat when they saw what they were to perform with, but Mac★★ash's consciousness-raising lecture working on their professional pride persuaded them to have a go regardless. The storyline was essentially domestic meloporn, with Girt's blissful wedding night with Jack threatened by the arrival of randy chamberperson Jock, until a new equilibrium is achieved by both men servicing the compaisant Girt, a reversal of the usual gender roles which Mac★★ash intended should alert audiences to her non-exploitative intent.

The first dipteran in the ointment was Jack's lamentable lack of potency. Whatever enticing postures Girt was levered into, however frantically Jack manipulated the offending member out of frame, the results were poor.

'This isn't supposed to be minimalism, for chrissake', Mac★★ash stormed from her director's chair. 'You're supposed to be the Come-shot Kid. What's the matter with you?'

'When they said I was to go with a real pig', Jack tried to explain, 'how was I to know they meant a real pig?'

Eventually Mac★★ash came up with the idea of using Jack's inability as part of the plot. Marriage night nerves on Jack's part would make Jock's intervention more welcome to Girt and more plausible to the audience. So Jack underwent the humiliation of colour closeups of his pitiful condition, with Girt on her flank giving a convincing performance of monumental disdain. He even submitted to putting his penis between Girt's jaws under threat of adverse publicity if he didn't.

'Besides', Mac★★ash said, 'she's been well fed, so there's absolutely no risk.'

Ashen-faced, Jack complied. Mac★★ash's only comment, she's merciless when she's working, was, 'Last ditch, no stand.'

When the day's shooting was over Jack tottered off to fortify himself with whisky and rhinoceros horn powder. Everyone else pronounced themselves well satisfied under the circumstances and looking forward to when Jock, who had been practising erections throughout the day in front of a mirror, would be on set.

The big seduction scene, the erotic heartland of the movie, was scheduled for first thing in the morning. Girt was lubricated like she was going to swim the Irish Sea, Jock was a coiled spring beneath his taut uniform, Mac★★ash, in an expansive mood, was passing out putative Oscars to cast and crew, while I, watching from on top of the dolly, was apprehensive.

At first it all went fine. Girt positively fluttered with coy anticipation as the handsome tray-bearing Jock leered down at her in bed next to the snoring groom, and then, as Jock unzipped to release Goliath, his pet name for it, but risky I'd have thought, she rolled over, won over, trotters skyward. The first camerawoman was placed downwind of the bed for a close-up of Goliath's purplish quarter metre slowly disappearing between Girt's quaking hams. The second camerawoman was craned up above, my point-of-view, for the balanced two-shot.

'Stand by number one for the come-shot', Mac★★ash directed, as Jock signalled. 'Number two close-up on Girt's face.'

With a strange keening sound, somewhere between the music our kind improvises preparatory to love and the thin clear whistle of falling bombs, Girt began to vocalize what we all assumed were the sounds of impending ecstasy.

'Fabulous. Spot on. This is art.'

But Girt was not crying joy, she was howling murder, so subsequent events proved, revenge for generations of her ancestors bred, fed, fattened and slaughtered, crimes she could detect wafting through the blood-stained seminal breath of the second son of a pork butcher. Girt's squeal hardened into sudden silence as her jaws clamped shut over the defenceless neck of her screen lover, severing the carotid artery.

Mac★★ash has been called many things for what she did next and for the sequence that testified to her action. While the two camerawomen leapt from their posts in a desperate attempt to staunch the flow without applying a lethal tourniquet, Mac★★ash seized the still running number one camera and, in a masterly pan, filmed the simultaneous emissions gouting from Goliath and its bearer's neck. By the time both gushers had died, Jock was dead meat.

'So they've got to send me a pig killer,' Mac★★ash commented to the press later, shaking her head in amazement. And then shaking it in sympathy, 'And to think Jack was worried about losing his prick.'

What I alone had seen from my vantage point over the blood-drenched mêlée was that Jack, fiction's cuckold and fact's failure, had, during the death agony of Jock, sprung to startling erectile life and would, is my surmise, had joyously consummated his marriage there and then had they not got a rope around Girt and hauled her off the deathbed. Some stories are better left untold. Jack has recently starred in a film produced by the hope of our national film industry, giving a performance that the critics are unanimous in proclaiming a unique assertion of the unquenchable spirit of Man.

No such plaudits came Pork's way after its legendary first and only showing as the centrepiece of our brandnew Prism Film Centre's opening ceremony. Amid the growing uproar, culminating in an attempt to storm the projection box, in which just she, I, and an intrepid projectionist on triple time were locked, it was evident that Mac★★ash's name was unspeakable. Sworn enemies were united now by common cause against the greater enemy: enemy of decency, of marriage, of the butcher's trade, of men, especially men, even of animals, and what more blameless creature than the pig. A nearby animal rights convention broke up in disarray as the word swept round the conference hall, with delegates vowing terrible vengeance on behalf of the exploited ungulate. Nor could the defence it was only a movie help her, because squirting semen and spurting blood were evidence it wasn't. Pork was snuff country. Worse, it was cunt snuffery. It was time for Mac★★ash to head for the hills to the east of our city.

Bunkered in a gully overhung by rowan, she pondered on the cruellest cut, the only one to have got through to the iron in her soul, made by those f-f-furious women who had charged her with betrayal. Above all, they had said, Pork stood for a hatred of the female gender. Mac★★ash vowed that unless this charge could be either repudiated or acknowledged she would never work again. Times were hard. She was eating catfood and I was hunting mice. At last she pronounced, 'They're right, and so am I – one third to two thirds. A little bit of self-hatred goes a long way. It's easy to become your own victim, your own worst enemy. My hands are none too clean, a pity they were not tied. So much for free expression. I need to work on something else. I'm fed up with eating out of tins. My cat hates living off the land. I'm coming back into town.'

And so we did. Soon after that she began working on a new script. Then our slow-cooking Association for the Generation of the Arts (AGA) came through with a production grant, and the shooting started. What it's about is difficult to deduce, but from the rushes I'd say it was an addition to the noir canon, suitably decked out with cinematic references, and in the approved arty style of the late '80s. I believe there may be a cat in it. It always helps to have something to identify with.

Three

Joyce, in the high tower, lifts her head from the maths of particle physics at the burst of cheering twenty stories down. It's our city's annual marathon, recharging the memory of victory over the Persians, no lone messenger today, several thousands already strung out by fitness/will differentials streaming past the pedestal of the tower. Among them, three friends. A bit of help from on high, Joyce punches a Persistence Furthers program into the mainframe console at her side, returns to work.

At the start we, Ursula and Samantha, were two out of three.

I, Dawn, missed the alarm, came to under the pull of their absence. Slipped into shorts, singlet, tracksuit, trainers reached the start to find them gone. Only persistence kept me going, catching the field, threading through under their guiding attraction. Nearer I got, the less the pull, the greater the effort.

We sensed her advance through the field, a pressure holding us back, lessening as she drew closer.

Then I was with them, and we were with her, running freely through the flux, equilibrated.

We gather from the pop papers we're three kinds of quark: up, down, sideways; charmed and, we submit, charming; each with her own colour, look at our tracksuits, Ursula red, Dawn green, Samantha blue; charged with energy, either $\frac{2}{3}e^+$ or $\frac{1}{3}e^-$; imbued, just one of us, with strangeness, that the others insist is me; bound together by the unbreakable elastic of gluons into the elementary particle Σ°.

Thirteen miles out the going got rough.

Another thirteen to go.

Imagine a joker leaping from his/her 4-by-13 pack to declaim: Another 26 to go, $\frac{1}{3}$ done, $\frac{2}{3}$ left, 39 in all. We'd kill him. Even her. No joke.

No joke, but around seventeen, feet numb, limbs on fire, rain stopped and a single bough of double cherry blossom reflecting in the glass façade of the Shanghai and Suburban

Bank mirrored by the water of the rockpool before it, all joy.

Nineteen, holding steady.

Into the twenty-third, my legs went, paralysing lassitude as if they'd been stripped of nerve and muscle. We sensed the sudden tug of her collapse, and stopped, while the field streamed past. Helped her to the roadside, rubbed calves and thighs, made her drink carbonated glucose solution.

I said, 'You must go on.'

We said, 'I can't go on.'

I said, 'I'll go on.'

After a mile with her helped hobbling between us, we broke once more into a run, up past real alehouses, cellar bars, renovated pubs, Irish bars, speakeasies, Chinese drinking clubs, supermarkets, emporia, hypermarts, kebab houses, Chinese takeaways, chai houses, Indian sweet centres, curry carry-outs, hot-dog stands, burger bars, pectopahs, diners, the Kentucky Fried Chicken, the Florida Fried Chicken, charcoal pits, grill 'n griddles, MacDonalds drive-in, slot-machine arcades, Golden Geese, Space Invaders, record shops, off-licences, liquor stores, berioshkas, radio stations, live music venues, video hires, discos, adult movies, pornshops, pawnshops, duty free shops, credit card facilities, cash dispensers, stripshows, peepshows, viewing booths, non-stop live action shows, cigarette kiosks, newspaper stands, advertising hoardings, massage parlours, saunas, jacuzzis, model agencies, French lessons upstairs, Swedish discipline upstairs, used car lots, multistory carparks, empty lots, minicab offices, automats, laudromats, police stations, security firms, bodyshops, sprayshops, tyres and exhausts, MOTs while-U-wait, self-drive carhire, chauffeur-driven carhire, gas stations, the Social Security offices, Job Centres, escort agencies, betting shops, casinos, tattooists and Chinese funeral parlours, until we came to the library, once round it, and then into Celebration Square, with the finishing line slung between the statues of Fred Engels and Georgie Best, the Monuments Committee being ultra-hot on getting such onetime residents ennobled in stone. .

We made it. I felt wonderful.

Inside the library, Persephone absent-mindedly notes the wave of cheering circling her hallowed rotunda. She has more important matters to attend to than a race against time.

One tiny fragment of today's project has been to track down, in response to a reader's enquiry that stubbornly resisted the efforts of her staff to answer it, the source of the term 'quark', which she has now established entered the lexicon in, and precisely where in, the Wake of Joyce.

Four

We women wove, in dreadful conditions and for low wages, the textiles to clothe their world. Our own backs were covered with coarse rough-weave hodden, kersey, duffle. Not for us the finer products of the loom.

At dawn, in the big house, the maids in their uniforms of dimity, calico, dowlas polished the silver and transported sir's urine downstairs for disposal. Not for them a celebration of their labour in song, that in your People's Republic was number one in '81: 'It gladdens my heart to hear the night-soil collectors coming down the mountain'.

Madam, in her shantung nightdress, delicately eased herself away from the still-damp patch on the linen where her husband's withdrawal had deposited his morning sperm, called for more lawn pillows to support her back and cushions of velours and plush on which to rest her feet that she might enjoy her breakfast in comfort. Not for her a radio-alarm to hoick her out of bed to do a five minute Jane Fonda workout before hauling on stretch pants and catching the bus to the office the temp agency's fixed up for this week.

The master in his weatherproof, thornproof, daresay bulletproof tweeds was up early to indulge in a day's shooting on the hills to the east of our city. Twill for the junior sportsmen, corduroy for the beaters. Not for them eight hour shifts at the monitor screens warning of nuclear attack in the bunker deep beneath the grouse-rich heather.

Madam debated which of her dresses she would wear today. In georgette, grosgraine, taffeta, jaconet, percale, tussore, gingham, paramatta, voile, organdie, tulle, lined with shalloon, mullmull, silesia and sarcanet, they paraded themselves for her delectation, a resplendent array of bright clear colours and softer subtler hues, whose textures took the light streaming through the open window and modified it, muted it, through an interminable play of ribbed, corded, twilled, raised, appliqué, gilded, knotted, worsted, napped, figured difference, inviting her decision this morning it would be the Balmain, to be borne to where she stood lovely in surah knic-

145

kers and Chantilly lace camisole by the devoted hand of her French maid, Bernadette. Not for Bernadette holidays in Ibiza, nor candlelit dinners at Luigi's, nor Harvey Wallbangers in the Chicago Diner paid for by her BMW-driving boyfriend whose dad's something big in insurance.

Young Master Rodney, pigging it in the country among the peasants for the weekend, where at least the grub was edible, plumped for the mohair suit in preference for the vicuña or alpaca, which he slipped on over his silk shirt and Windsor-knotted foulard tie. He believed in style, and style dictated swansdown for his socks, moleskin for his gloves and seersucker for his handkerchiefs. Not for him a glimmer of doubt as to his innate right to never work.

Miss Amanda, eager to get some practice in before the afternoon's tennis party, took a cashmere woollie just in case the cambric of her frock was not proof against the morning chill. Dilthey wore printed nainsook, so unbecoming on the court, but you couldn't really complain seeing how she'd given up her morning off to spend it returning one's serves. Not for either of them to play the cotton futures in our city's Exchange, the great game of making money.

My sister, my mother and I all worked in the mill until it closed down, redundant, and us with it. Soon after that my sister developed an inoperable tumour. We nursed her during her slow, pitiful decline towards death. Then my mother's health, weakened by years of breathing dust, also gave way, and after a brief hot summer when it seemed she was getting better, she died the following winter of emphysema. I was nineteen and a half. During the years that followed I found other employment, went to night school, studied ferociously, won a scholarship to university, became a journalist, got married to a decent intelligent man, bore three children, and have become, in my late middle years, a prolific if financially precarious writer of popular fiction. I am aware of the ironies of my occupation. Millgirl turned writer, what I was and what I am are not so far apart as might commonly be supposed. Though the form in which my labour is purchased may differ from what it was, my product is equally not mine to sell or control. A publisher's contract may delay its surrender in a way that the wage contract never does, yet both products are commodities offered for sale by those other than their makers. As a writer my income is more directly linked to the success of the company's marketing strategy than it is as a millgirl, but that is all. Of more interest to me, though, than such analogies in the realm of production is the uncanny resemblance of the products, of which the common root of the words 'text' and 'textile' is the clue. The Latin verb 'texere' means 'to weave'. The threads crisscross to make the cloth of language, which then as tailor and seamstress too I cut and stretch to make what others will adopt for their social requirements. I worry about the quality of my stuff, popular though, as, it may be. The best as ever goes to those who can afford it. I try not to sacrifice quality to cost, but if I were to write what I would like I would only be making luxury goods for those with cultural capital in the bank. My experience as a wage labourer made me sensitive to contradictions. The political education I got from my sister warns me that power is never ceded voluntarily. My mother's example suggests to me that the choice of right over ease involves inevitable hardship. So in spinning my yarn about a not-so-frail frail with a cat I'm mindful of who will or will not wear its eventual fabric.

Five

It's a matter of rational reconstruction from the fragments about the place. The bit which would give the myth its point would seem to be missing. We've pursued it in the library, hunting through the catalogue, prowling down the alleys between the tiered shelves, even gaining audience with the Librarian who conceded she had once heard something to that effect but could not recall the source. It is something that exists by rumour only. One authority cites a reference to a text which when tracked down omitted all mention of it. Yet the pursuit itself generates hints, by themselves signifying nothing yet in combination with the rest suggesting . . . . a resistance, a cover-up. It is impossible to pin anything down, but our suspicion of a plot thickens as the coincidences mount up. Yesterday, for instance, having just read of the cat-goddess Bast, we turned on the TV and immediately heard mention of one Frau Bast in Fassbinder's Berlin Alexanderplatz. There is nothing particularly to connect Bast with Osiris, nor any direct evidence that it was a cat that made off with and ate his member. His reconstruction from the other dozen fragments of his morcellated body had perforce to remain incomplete through the irretrievability of the thirteenth part. As god of the underworld he might have been able to get by without it, though the devil is portrayed with two or even three. Absence or excess, there seems to be no golden mean. Then the Osiris-Orpheus linkage, and the Orpheus-Actaeon, are extraordinarily imprecise. The myths of a continent, so says my jeans manufacturer, exist only as their many versions, none of them original or conclusive. Ours of Oedipus has its Viennese and Hellenic variants, in which castration or sightlessness are but the expression of temperamental differences between the centre and the south. In any case, our temperamental bias, as woman and cat, is towards another with dogs, a specific difference that excites our interest. The fact Actaeon got torn to pieces by Diana's hounds after watching her bathe at a pool in a glade in the forest is of less import than the familiar relationship. If narrative, with its plot-obsessed paranoia, asks that we get to the point, we reply that that surely is what is at stake. All right, yielding, we'll render our northern variant so long as it and you concede our right to deviate.

So there was this boy, lived in the prosperous suburbs, got given by his parents for his fourteenth birthday a telescope, Haley's Met Series, 700 roubles at unofficial exchange rates, with a thick crimson barrel and molybdo-chrome eyepiece, that for the first lunar month was angled at the stars. After this the boy lowered it and began spying on his neighbours.

Of the dozen or so houses his augmented vision could penetrate past flowering laburnum trees and net curtains three, successively, fired his curiosity. The first stood in the boy's mind for the life of the mind. In its richly decorated and book-lined rooms there lived alone an elderly man with a limp, who ate at the head of an empty table and spent much of his time writing at a large antique desk or reading in a leather armchair. In the second house, which stood for the life of the spirit, there lived an enormous family comprising a grandmother, her two daughters and a son-in-law, several grandchildren and their innumerable pets, who all had a constant stream of visitors, with the result that late into every night there would emanate the sounds of laughter, argument, early rock and roll, and the distinctive clicking of Mah Jong tiles. Both these houses were across the avenue from him, but some way down it in opposite directions, so that the angle of vision was such that over half of what took place in them was barred to his sight.

But the house that fascinated him the most, and time and again drew him relentlessly to his telescope, directly backed on to his own, beyond the privet hedge at the bottom of the garden, and offered perfect visibility. In it there lived a woman of about thirty with her somewhat older husband, who seemed to fade into the background as if he wasn't there, and indeed wasn't a lot of the time, often being away for two or three days on end. Then the woman would be alone in the house except for the two lean, brindled, fearsome Rottweilers who were her constant companions. This woman's blonde voluptuousness, which at first had struck the boy as excessive, soon began to induce in him a barely controllable longing to look at her. She was inclined to lie around the house in clothes more suited, he thought, to Majorca than to our city, halter tops in bright nylon, tight-fitting pink cotton pants, loose diaphanous pyjama-type outfits with low necklines revealing her heavy, free-swinging breasts. She did little but eat, read magazines, and romp with the dogs from time to time, apart, that is, from what the boy referred to as 'attending to her person'. This last, in full view through the plateglass picture window of her open-plan lounge, or upstairs in her bedroom, sited by some stroke of fortune at the back of the house, evidently gave her and indubitably gave him many hours of pleasure. Sometimes, after a session at the telescope, his whole face ached with the strain of keeping one eye shut and the other open. He would happily ignore such discomfort for the joy of watching her paint her toenails scarlet or, at weekends, heliotrope, and when dry draw on butterfly-motif tights up her extended leg with the foot carefully pointed, first one, then the other; or of watching her make herself up, seated at her bedroom dressing table, a ritual succession of rouge, eye shadow, eye pencil, and a double application of lip gloss, cyclamen margined with madder. But what excited him most was when she bathed. The Venetian blind covering her bathroom window became a source of almost unbearable anticipation as to whether it would be pulled right up, as it was during her daytime baths, or whether if down, as it was at night, the slats would be horizontal, with her clearly visible in the artificially lit bathroom, or inclined, so removing her from his insatiable gaze. In time the boy came to know every detail of her toilet. He saw her wash her hair, rubbing the shampoo into a rich white crown of lather, then tilt her head back to rinse it off under the steaming jets from the shower. He saw her step from the bath and wrap herself in a huge white towel, then wind another smaller one around her head in a turban. He saw her dry herself, beginning with her feet while she leant forward over the bath, then moving up her legs and over her thighs until she reached the peach-coloured thicket on her lower belly, then her weighty buttocks, her torso and breasts, arms and shoulders. He watched her rub deodorant under her arms, shake powder on her thighs, anoint her breasts with oils, and touch perfume to the pulse of her wrists and neck. He watched her towel her hair, then shake it out between her fingers, to fall loosely on to her shoulders. And then on rare and wonderful occasions he watched her walk from bathroom to uncurtained bedroom, where she would put on silken underwear, select a dress, slip it over her head, stand contemplating her image before a mirror, perhaps take off the dress and select another until she had the measure of her satisfaction and would then turn from the mirror to fasten the zip, slide her feet into a pair of matching high-heeled shoes, and descend the stairs to where her dogs would be yelping a welcome. This house represented the life of the body.

'I knew straightaway I was being watched. The dogs knew it too, warning me with their low-pitched growling something was up. It didn't take too long to spot him and his telescope. My first impulse was to hand the little tyke over to the police. But he was only a kid and that seemed a bit much. Probably give him a complex or something. Before I did anything I figured I'd anyway give him his money's worth. So I played up a bit, laid it on thick. He must have loved it. The dogs didn't though, sensed I was up to something. Listen you mutts, I told them, you take me as I come or you're going to get it. That quieted them, but I could hear them simmering. With dogs like that you're on top or you're nowhere. One snap from those jaws and your throat is clean out. Maurice won't go near them when I'm not around. Maybe that's why he was away so much, off selling his software. I toyed with the idea of payng a social call on his parents and hinting to him that I knew what he was up to. Or else phoning up and just breathing down the phone when he answered it. Or else getting a telescope and pointing it right back at him. But I didn't, more's the pity. None of those things. I just let him carry on looking. But I also didn't, whatever anyone says, leave the door on the latch deliberately. First sign of anything wrong was a draft upstairs, and I realized the dogs had got out the back. Then I heard the screams. They went on for maybe thirty seconds, while I rushed downstairs and out into the garden, calling for Granger and Wild Thing. Then it suddenly went quiet. They slunk back into the house a minute or so later, spattered with blood and foam around their mouths. Then came the wail of a police siren, followed by an ambulance. I could see their blue lights flashing in front of his house. I can still see that blue in my mind's eye. The dogs just curled up and went to sleep. It was the last thing they ever did, the poor bastards.'

Somehow they stitched the boy back together again, even managed, with the latest micro-surgical techniques, to sew on the little finger of his left hand that he had lost in his struggle to ward off his attackers. They found that under the sofa. After three months in hospital he emerged with only lines of suture and some scar tissue around his eyes to show for his ordeal. The boy was all of a piece. The only thing missing in the whole affair, as he discovered when he got home, was his telescope. Of its possible fate nobody said anything, least of all the boy and to this day its whereabouts remains a mystery. The idea of replacing it didn't occur to him. All technology of vision had become repellent, to the extent that he even refused to go to the cinema or to watch television. When questioned about this aversion, he'd mutter, 'No more images for this kid'. His parents professed bafflement, but were secretly pleased, being of the opinion he'd always been keener on spectacle than was good for him. It was an ill wind that blowed nobody any good and if this ghastly accident had cured him of that then perhaps this was the price of growing up. The boy didn't know about growing up, but felt, as he put it, 'Dead empty', or even just plain, 'Dead'. He roamed listlessly through the sightless underworld they called maturity for what seemed like years, which was probably only weeks, but may possibly have been decades, until eventually, in despair, he picked up a book at random and began to read. At first the words were like braille to a blinded man, harsh awkward things, laden with brute materiality, incapable of conveying sense, suffused with darkness. Gradually, however, their baffling, arbitrary leadenness eased, and they began to proffer meaning, giving form and substance to the world his accident had consigned him to. He found now there were certain advantages to his condition. In any case there was no question of his returning to the primitive delight of looking. That was irreparably lost. On the other hand his underworld conferred a freedom he'd never previously known, not of his own choosing exactly, yet present in the necessity of what was written. He found such thoughts difficult to articulate. His reading took him into realms of difference, unimagined and unimaginable, though some of them were imaginary. The boy learned to live with paradoxes. As he read of our city so he was able to avail himself of its many realities, among them the library, where we too have had occasion to browse. One day within its portals he encountered Persephone, a woman of a similar age but different colouring to that other whom he now only recalled as through a glass darkly. The story of Persephone and the boy, unfolding through the seven waystations of knowledge, as he came to call her by her seven names, is one we would like to relate, and may yet.

Six

Besides their dogs the General and La Jefe have in common a granddaughter each, whom they hope will inherit and administer not only their respective establishments in our city but also the obtuse-angled slice of voting stock the General holds in IOU (International Operations Unlimited) and La Jefe in FF&F (Fish, Forestry and Finance), corporations whose competitive hemispheric interface becomes increasingly abrasive as time rolls by. Some hope. The General's has been with the Wobblies since she was fourteen, took Engels to bed with her throughout her adolescence while other girls of her age were vying to do the same with Georgie Best, and goes on holidays in the relatively autonomous further republics of the US of R, next year a canoeing trip down the Ussuri River doing her bit for socialist unity. As for La Jefe's, she's so deeply into feminity it's like ~~Angkor Wat on a steamy night with flares lighting up the chirruping jungle and somewhere someone's talking of a fat tropical snail that's crawling unseathed along the edge of a razor blade.~~ Not at all the girls to handle their grannies' corporate rationality.

Their manifestoes.

$Anna_1$'s.

> Terminal state of late capitalism. Domination of global economy by transnationals. Constant threat of falling profits, bankruptcies, takeovers. Need to export capital from metropolitan countries in search for lower costs. Third World economies impoverished by debt incurred to pay for investment to counter monopoly penetration. Financial instability resulting from unrestrained liquidity flows following collapse of Bretton Woods. Threat to banking system upon repudiation of debt. De-industrialization of sectors of metropolitan economies leading to political unrest requiring internal repression. Increasing commodification of sectors of the economy previously outside of capitalist production. Most buoyant sectors of industrialized economies those with least use

value, notably arms production. Soviet threat concocted to justify such expenditure and to contain internal opposition. Loss of imperialist control of areas of globe to local nationalisms, decreasing opportunities for investment. Grandma's IOU into debt. US hegemony threatened by European and especially Japanese penetration of markets. Effective wartime economy increasingly only means of staving off depression. Multiplying contradictions raise likelihood of military confrontation between US and USSR. Possibility of physical annihilation of competing capitalist economies through local nuclear wars in Europe and Far East. Opportunities for reconstruction as basis for renascent US economy. Limit possibility of capitulation by Soviet Union with attendant economic and political expansion by US. Resistance by Soviet Union to intimidation. Resistance by national liberation struggles, anti-imperialist struggles and non-aligned and socialist regimes. Internal metropolitan opposition by labour movement, civil rights movement, disarmament campaigns, environmentalist groups, women's movement, minorities campaigns, anti-fascist alliances, regionalism, separatism, and cultural subversion.

And Anna$_2$'s.

Multiply mutilated mujeres waging anti-phallogocentric terror from deep within the labial zone. Skulls ringing to primal mothering inscriptions. Jouissance traversing the body politic. Patriarchal institutions destabilized by lactating cadres proffering illogic, intuition, ephemerality, compassion and magic. Children everywhere. Aunties conducting learning–is–forgetting teach-ins. Total nonstop global telephone conversation among all women following conversion of granma's FF&F from phalloidal figuration into feminist phratry. Power secreted along invisible channels, in beds, kitchens, labour wards, stripclubs, biscuit factories, primary schools, WI meetings, hotel corridors, airport lounges, hairdressing salons, mental institutions. Difference articulated in languages undevised by men. Resonance. Cellular division. Glossolalia. Elaborate new topologies of body and mind. The White House pink. The Kremlin saffron yellow. No locks, no property, no paternity. No money, no insurance, no banks. Poignant ecstasies of particularities, chance encounters, coincidences. Ecological balance. Plants from tropical rainforests cultivated to satisfy nutrutional and medicinal needs. Fish swimming in profusion in the oceans, swallows diving through insect-laden late evening summer air. Music. Laughter. The great door of pleasure flung wide open for evermore.

In reply, a joint communiqué from the General and La Jefe, issued by Clara McGibbon, press officer of the Chihuahua Club.

Burying our corporate and personal differences in common cause against the revolutionism and subversion of our two female descendants, we wish to state our view that the order we control represents the highest stage of human development, with unprecedented opportunities for individuals of all classes, genders, races, religions and nationalities to advance and succeed. In comparison with all other existing social orders, past and present, ours, underwritten by democracy and the scientific outlook, is by far and away the freest, most prosperous, most varied and most open to change. Other regimes putting themselves forward as alternatives can offer only stifling conformity, bureaucratic rule, economic inefficiency, intolerance, over-politicization, obscurantism, hysteria or paranoia. Revolutionism always descends from its abstract notion of universal justice to concrete injustices of a kind that are more extreme and harder to eradicate than those found within conservative regimes. As for feminism, its rational components are perfectly compatible with our politics of advancement for individuals and groups, while its fundamentalist call to replace so-called patriarchy with a would-be matriarchy resuscitates the worst, most demeaning stereotype of women as irrational beings and rests upon a dangerous identification of men as the cause of women's discontent. In conclusion, a significant if unorthodox index of the maturity of our present system is the election to highest office and subsequent impressive performance of a onetime film actor. In a world where such a thing can happen what limits are there to people's aspirations?

Now for some cinema.

In four different scenarios – one each – the granddaughters and their grandmothers are clipclopping along under the towering mesas of Monument Valley / sprawled on chairs and a bed in a hotel room lit by a bare bulb and the flicker of a faulty neon sign outside in the rainswept Philadelphia street / seated around a polished table in a boardroom perched high in the Manhattan sky / in a car driving fast along the winding coast road north of Big Sur.

'Cut!'

The General reins her horse to a sudden halt / savagely stubs out a cigarette in the already full ashtray / stalks to the plate-glass window and turns in silhouette against the skyline / slams on the brakes.

'Cut!'

An arrow flies over their heads and plunges into a cactus behind them / there's a loud banging on the hotel room door / the telephone rings / a black sedan draws up alongside.

'Cut!'

With a clatter of hooves a Navajo scout gallops towards them, hands a roll of parchment to La Jefe, and rides off in a cloud of dust / the door opens and a seedy little man played by Elisha Cook Jnr comes in, thrusts an envelope into La Jefe's hand, and scuttles out with a nervous glance over his shoulder / La Jefe makes a grab for the phone, listens intently for a while, jots something down on a notepad, and replaces the receiver / a window of the black sedan is rolled down, a hand reaches out and passes a piece of paper to La Jefe in the back seat, then the car accelerates away in a screech of tyres.

'Cut!'

La Jefe hands to the General the roll of parchment / the envelope / the notepad / the piece of paper.

Anna$_1$ and Anna$_2$: What does it say?

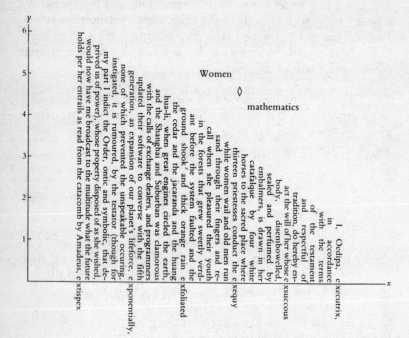

Seven

Women

mathematics

I, Oedipa, executrix, in accordance with the terms of the testament and respectful of tradition, do hereby enact the will of her whose executrix body, disembowelled, sealed and perfumed by embalmers, is drawn in her catafalque by four white horses to the sacred place where thirteen priestesses conduct the exequy while women wail and old men run sand through their fingers and recall when she pleasured their youth in the forests that grew sweetly verdant before the system faulted and the ground shook, and thick orange rain exfoliated the cedar and the jacaranda and the huang hua-li, when great engines circled the earth, and the Shanghai and Suburban was clamorous with the calls of exchange dealers, and programmers updated their software to converse with the fifth generation, an expansion of our planet's lifeforce, none of which prevented the unspeakable occurring, instigated, it is rumoured, by the testator (though for my part I indict the Order, ontic and symbolic, that deprived us of power), whose property disposed of as she wished, would now have me broadcast to the multitude what the future holds per her entrails as read from the catacomb by Amadeus, extispex

Eight

'F-f-fakes, f-f-forgeries, f-f-fabrications.'

The burghers' outrage froths and spumes about the curator as she saunters past humidifiers cutting out puzzled by the sudden increase in atmospheric moisture. Not her that's sweating, they figure, must be the Friends. Well wouldn't you be, goes the word along the automatic blinds, if you'd ladled out sponsorship to save who knows how many billion lire worth of Sienese Master from going to the Coast, only to find these six Matisses at less than a G apiece, canvas and paint included, ogling you every time you checked your investment. It's a disgrace, snaps a photo-electric eye, a scandal of art international proportions. The colloquy of things buzzes on. Here's our City Gallery, modest by the standards of the Met down the road or the Hermitage up it, setting a precedent that could wreck the market. Only the top two or three Matisse-men can tell these from their originals bunkered behind bullet-proof glass, fronted by Kalashnikov-toting Securicop hit-men. For most of us city folk taking time off work if we've got it to recreate ourselves in the Gallery's lambent spaces, they're the real thing, or as good as, or better. As for those who want the curator hung next to them, turning the world upside down like this, they just have to take what the turnstile counter tells them, that each has its inauthenticity clearly labelled, stating where the original is to be found, when the copy was made, and whose hand it was that painstakingly traced it.

When pressed by journalists and critics, the curator, elegant in a white linen suit and pearls, admonishes, 'Let the paintings speak for themselves.'

So the hacks, coughing, stumble back and listen.

'The question of "copyright", despite or because of its marginal or extra-textual place (but one which is never simply anywhere, since, were the © absolutely detached, it would lose all value), should no longer be evaded in any of its aspects, be they legal, economical, political, ethical, phantasmatic, or libidinal.'

'Ultimately, there is only a tactile vitality comparable to the vibrato of the violin or voice.'

$$'y = x^2 - x^4$$

'Pictures which have become refinements, subtle gradations, dissolutions without energy, call for beautiful blues, reds, yellows – matters to stir the sensual depths in men.'

'Meaning is but little to these men; all they care for is line, shape, agreement of contour. They are given up to the pleasure principle.'

'An artist must possess Nature. He must identify himself with her rhythm, by efforts that will prepare the mastery which will later enable him to express himself in his own language.'

'We seek out woman, all of us – women or men – desiring to overcome the gap separating the sexes, to take part in a linking of tresses that for each of us can join him or her, outside and inside, reality and sign.'

$$'y = xe^{-x}'$$

'Murder, death, and unchanging society represent precisely the inability to hear and understand the signifier as such – as ciphering, as rhythm, as a presence that precedes the signification of object or emotion.'

'Hatred, rancour and a vengeful disposition are burdens which the artist cannot load upon himself.'

'But chromatic experience casts itself as a turning point between the "self's" conservative and destructive proclivities; it is the place of narcissistic eroticism (autoeroticism) and death drive – never one without the other.'

'If we are not to abandon the hypothesis of the death instincts, we must suppose them to be associated from the very first with the life instincts.'

This lameness I feign
Your bounty to gain
And not that to limp is a pleasure:
Then acquit me from blame,
If I choose to be lame
Nor censure me thus without measure;
For if people complain,
My excuse I maintain,
"It is lawful to limp for a treasure".

$$'y = \sqrt{x^2 - 1}'$$

Ich hinke, doch nicht aus Vergnügen am Hinken,
Ich hink' um zu essen, ich hink' um zu trinken.
Ich hinke, wo Sterne der Hoffnung mir winken,
Ich hinke, wo Gulden entgegen mir blinken.
Was man nicht erfliegen kann, muß man erhinken.
Viel besser ist hinken, als völlig zu sinken.
Die Schrift sagt: Es ist keine Sünde zu hinken.

$$'y = x^x'$$

تعارجْتُ لا رغبةً في آلعرجْ   ولكـِـن إِذا رَعَ باتُ آلفـرجْ
وأُلقـَي حبْلي على غـارِبي   وأسْلُكَ مَسْلكَ منْ قدْ مرجْ
فإن لامني آلقوْمُ قُلْتُ آعْذِرُوا   فـلَيس على أعْرجَ منْ حرجْ

Impressed, the tribe of scribes troop out, their notebooks crammed with usable copy. One, fortunate enough to have graph paper interleaved in his spiral notebook, has sketched the functions, in so far as this is possible, encouraged by those clustered interestedly around him. Another knot is arguing attributions, just which said what and when, not that their editors will give a monkey's, but there is always professional pride. Then there's the little matter of what the printers will make of the squiggles, better tell them it's shorthand or they'll want to negotiate a special rate for the job. And to think, says someone quoting Rock, as far as I was concerned Art was just a guy's name.

In the silence that falls, the curator, Sandra Jewel, with one l, contemplates the paintings. Loretta With White Turban returns her gaze with a dispassionate stare, her dress wrapped closely to her body, the pink of the chair duskily repeated across her belly. Interior With Gramophone permits a glimpse of the painter, in a mirror framed by the curtain pulled to one side with a cord, behind a table bearing fruit. With shackling anklets of topaz and jade, mathematically curvaceous, offering languid invitation to her owner, the female slave of Odalisque: Harmony In Red makes the curator see red, so emblematic is it of the ineluctable chaining of women through desire. As for the Woman With Umbrella, her feeling is, come rain or shine, folded or unfolded, who needs one? Still-life With Fruit, decoratively floral, enables her to assert that where there's still life there's a hope something may be done, and the pleasure of its colour field is intense. From the last, Nude On Ornamental Ground, she infers translations from east to west, but the spare, sandy angularity of the woman's body against the complexity of the carpet and drape unsettles her judgement as to its meaning.

Nine

With black eyes glittering and black cape flapping Librarian Birdwissel circumambulated her rotunda, insomniac, incorruptible. After the revolution no library, least of all our city's, would ever be the same again. The system she envisaged would bring to an end the prehistory of librarianship and would usher in its true history. The existing order, with its categories, subjects, alphabetizisation, index cards, author catalogues, title catalogues, digests, bibliographies, stacks and shelves, would become a memory, and then would be forgotten altogether. In contrast to her time-serving colleagues she had welcomed computerization in the clear understanding that it provided the means to achieve her end. Whereas the Mensheviks on the Management Committee viewed the IBM 7000 in the basement as at best an opportunity to consolidate their shortsighted rationality, she knew it was the ally of a truly democratic regime of reader power. When, in April, she submitted her theses to the Committee, they reacted with predictable horror. By midsummer, despite a reactionary attempt to get her dismissed, she had painstakingly met their every objection and was able to muster an overall majority in favour. Three months later, in early October, following frenzied nonstop overtime by the programmers and other staff, Librarian Birdwissel decreed that the hour of reader-power had come.

No.

The nine hundred classificatory numbers with their embedded subdivisions were obliterated by a randomization device. P. O. Birdwissel, D. Litt., decreed that every book have its number removed, and be taken from the shelves which were then to be dismantled and sold for scrap. Instead of occupying a 3-dimensional shelf space derived from a classificatory n-space, each book now took its chance in a composite stochastic multivariate set in heaps on the floor. One book might be next to another, or on top of it, because of their covers being both yellow, for instance, or because of the same typeface, or because they each opened with the same word, or because both had a reference to Borges in the index, or for any one of an infinitude of discernible reasons, or for no reason at all.

No.

On Monday morning, when the library opened, Ms Birdwissel ranged through its re-organized halls, watching for readers' responses and eager to see how they would utilize their newfound freedom. They seemed, however, reluctant to do so, and throughout the day her staff were besieged with enquiries from the public as to how to find the books they wanted. All such enquiries were to be answered with the words: Begin where you like, one book will lead to the next, don't worry. At the end of the day, just before closing time, the library staff met and unanimously passed a motion condemning what had taken place and withdrawing their labour from the Libraries Department of our city until such time as the situation was reversed. Ms Birdwissel accused them of treachery, but to no avail. The next morning there were pickets outside the entrance to the library. During the course of the day just three people ventured past the picket line, a tramp in search of warmth, an Iranian student, and a married woman on a clandestine assignation. Each drifted through the library without so much as touching a book. Even the Iranian student, researching the many tyrannies his country had known, left shortly before midday, while the others, finding neither warmth, for the heating was off, nor faint-hearted lover, had gone by eleven. At eight o'clock in the evening, the porters, who belonged to a different union and were not on strike, prepared to shut up. Ms Birdwissel informed them that she would be staying behind. The door closed, with her alone inside the library and everyone else in the world outside.

No.

As she wandered through the echoing spaces contemplating the disorder she had been instrumental in bringing about, Persephone Birdwissel, for the first time in many years, wept. She understood that in undoing the categories by which knowledge is organized she had done more than bring the library to a standstill, and as the night wore on she had a terrible suspicion as to what this might be. Around midnight, she removed the pass key of the main door of the library

166

from her pocket and inserted it apprehensively into the lock. As the door swung open she saw that every trace of our city had vanished. A grey mist swirled wetly in around her, bringing with it a faint but unmistakable smell of unwashed socks. That seemed to be all. Tentatively she put a foot over the threshold and encountered some sort of resistance that might conceivably be ground. Uncaring now, she stepped out into the fog, and after a few paces was utterly swallowed up by it. Nor was the library visible any longer. The only thing to do was to continue walking. After a while she heard a slight buzzing coming from some indeterminate place, and a little later shapes loomed up indiscernibly in her peripheral vision, only to merge once more into the mist as she turned to approach them. She felt like a sponge floating in dirty bathwater gone cold. After several hours of this she heard a voice calling.

No.

At which point Persephone understood that she existed only by virtue of being an idea in the mind of another. She was a fiction within a text in which an unknown author expressed his, less probably her, imaginings, and was liable to disappear at any moment into the terminal extinction of the wastepaper basket. She underwent a terror such as she would not have believed possible. In the midst of her terror she had the thought, or rather, as she now supposed, the thought was given to her, that one chance, horribly slim, of survival might be to secure the collaboration of her author. If she could do a deal, then he might be persuaded to permit her to return from limbo, or wherever it was she was stuck. The only conceivable enticement she could offer was to exchange her fiction of him for his of her. As an imaginary woman it might be appropriate to present a life made up of such. Some women, of course, were more imaginary than others, but the time for niceties was long gone. Her librarian's experience would be invaluable, although in recalling the fictions that were to be the facts of his life she felt there was a certain slippage in her memory, as if her mind was succumbing to the disorienting effects of sensory deprivation. She must hurry, if she was to succeed. The fog seemed to be thickening around her. Coming to a standstill, she lifted her head and cried to whoever might be listening,

> *Miranda* by William Shakespeare,
> *Candida* by François-Marie Voltaire,
> *Emma* by Jane Austen,
> *Dorothea* by George Eliot,
> *Anna* by Leo Tolstoy,
> *Virginia* by Mrs Dalloway,
> *Livia* by James Joyce,
> *Margherita* by Mikhail Bulgakov,
> *Rebecca* by Daphne du Maurier,
> *Clea* by Laurence Durrell,
> *Ada* by Vladimir Nabokov,
> *Oedipa* by Thomas Pynchon.

Was this sufficient to ensure her survival?

No.

The extremities of her body began to merge into the mist, a dissolution matching the fragmentation of her mind into shards of dissociated will and idea. Into the murk she howled in defiance the name of one last text, a terminal supplement to her list, the thirteenth,

> *Angelica* by P. Birdwissel,

a romance she had written in her late infancy. The results were remarkable. In front of her there wafted down, like an immense discarded outer lettuce leaf, what she instantly saw was the corpse of the author in whose text she imagined she belonged. Picking it up she could see it was comprised of no more than crumpled and rather soggy pieces of paper mashed into a sort of provisional cohesion, some of them blank, others covered with a blurred scrawl. The fog was lifting, blown by a breeze smelling of artificial violets, certainly preferable to dirty socks. She appeared to be on a rough track, with a steep shaly slope down on one side and nearly sheer cliff on the other. As she rounded a bend there loomed into view the unmistakable dome of the library she knew so well. Presumably her path through the fog had taken her in a circle to finish up where she had begun. With relief bordering on ecstasy at her reprieve, she reached for the key that would open the familiar door and restore her once again to her domain. There were revisions called for, she could appreciate that now, to the system she had inaugurated. Possibly, as a beginning, the restoration of shelves?

No.

Per saw that the door was not as it should have been. Instead of a keyhole on the left there was an eight-spoked wheel in the dead centre, which remained immobile whichever way she tried to turn it. The door itself was covered with interlocking inscriptions in various languages, giving a curious three-dimensional effect. It was as if the door itself were an immense rebus, yielding up fragments of meaning that dissolved back into a shifting kaleidoscope of alternatives whenever she tried to hold on to one of them. Once again she wrenched the eight-spoked wheel as hard as she could to left and right, but it resisted all her efforts. It did seem though, following her exertions, that the play of meaning inherent in the rebus became even more exuberant, a fizzing cascade of transient significances, each with its own particular emotional colour. If this was the door, Per thought during a brief lull in the firework party, what on earth or off it could possibly lie beyond? Might it not even be that the door was all there was, unopenable and impassable, leading on to nothing, neither library nor anything else? Faced by such questions it would have been easy enough to resign herself to waiting for something to happen, in the time honoured tradition of heroines, but Per hadn't become a revolutionary librarian without subscribing to a philosophy of action. Feeling around inside her shoulder bag she discovered what from the label could only be a stick of dynamite, though she could have sworn she hadn't put it there. What is more, she also found a book of matches, inscribed with her initials P.O.B., in the lining of her jacket, despite being a non-smoker. Never one to miss an opportunity, she positioned the dynamite securely between the eight-spoked wheel and the door, struck a match, lit the fuse and ran to a convenient sheltering rock. The explosion, when it came, was unimpeachable and about twice as loud as her training would have led her to expect. Letters, part-words, bits of sentences showered past her to smash up against the cliff behind or roll down the slope into the valley. And there, curving through the air in a high trajectory, was the eight-spoked wheel, now minus a spoke, the cause of all the difficulty. She peered over the top of her rock through the hole where the door had been to what lay beyond, which seemed to be a continuation of the track she was on. Then, as the smoke cleared, she saw a figure peering over the top of a similarly placed rock on the far side. With a feeling of intense excitement, Per stood up and began walking through the residual dust towards him, less probably her. This other, who had grey–blue eyes and was naturally wearing a tracksuit, after a slight yet incontrovertible time-lag, also stood up and began advancing towards Per.

Ten

The trail leads back to Hermes Trismegistus, 'the friend of whoever is lonely', adviser to Osiris, where all further traces vanish. This Hermes, it seems, authored the text from which the major arcana of six times thirteen Tarot cards derive. Then in 1958, a single shot from Touch of Evil of a scattered Tarot figures the question of the future put by sheriff Hank Quinlan to Tanya, madame of a Los Robles whorehouse, played with stunning effect by Marlene Dietrich in a black wig. She tells him, 'You haven't got any.' 'What?' he grunts, 'What do you mean?' She means, 'Your future is all used up.' The film is commonly acknowledged to be the last film noir, a cycle started by The Maltese Falcon in 1941, Pearl Harbour year, that depicts male anxiety in the face of the threat posed by women. The fat man in the former is Sydney Greenstreet's ebullient Gutman, compulsively questing for the black bird which turns out, of course, to be a fake, so giving him and his associates the excuse to renew the search for the elusive original. Welles' obese, corrupt Quinlan is sustained by no such object of desire, having irrevocably lost it to the past. Between these two, a third extra–cinematic Fat Boy was dropped on Hiroshima, so placing The Maltese Falcon in one era and Touch of Evil in another.

Memory of the frame,

discerns the identity of some, but not all, of the cards shown. The two identifiable within the top right group are the queen of wands and the knight of pentacles, described as respectively symbolizing 'a blued-eyed, flaxen-haired woman, domestic, companionable, honourable and chaste' and 'a black-haired, brown-eyed young man, worldly-wise and methodical'. Spectators will have no problem recognizing Janet Leigh's Susan and her husband, Charlton Heston's Mexican drugs investigator Mike Vargas. Their identities are confirmed by the isolated card between them, the two of cups, signifying 'a spiritual union. . . partnership, harmony, co-operation, engagement'. Mike and Susan are newly weds. So far, so good: one theme of the film is their forcible separation and eventual reunification. Vargas' investigation also exposes Quinlan as a framer and murderer, culminating in his downfall and death. The group of cards on the lower left should therefore encapsulate this other theme. There should in particular be a card representing Quinlan, and indeed prominent among them is the king of wands, 'a man of enterprise and power'. He is, however, 'honest and conscientious and can also be passionate and noble', a judgement that at first sight would be at odds with what is known of Quinlan, until it is recalled that it is his dedicated pursuit of crime, sustained by the memory of his own wife, dead by strangling, that makes him ignore the legal requirements of evidence. The interpretation just about holds. But then it goes awry, refusing to align itself with the plot. Most visible among the other cards of the group are the eight of pentacles and the ace of cups, standing for 'an artist at his craft, which he exhibits' and 'great abundance'. The first must refer to Welles as director of the film, so diverting attention from meaning to the conditions for the production of meaning and, within this expanded textual field, the second might refer to the process of interpretation itself, prolix and joyous. Nevertheless, according to Tanya's precognition, there should be adjacent to the king of wands another card, the scythe-wielding figure on horseback, the reaper, Death. It is not present.

On the radio a newsflash breaks in to announce that Orson Welles, hoaxer, actor, auteur, advertiser, charmer, magician, has died in Hollywood aged 70. It would seem that the realm of the interpretable, like gravity, like levity, is co-extensive with the world. The reader has become the reaper. Requiem for the Kenosha Kid.

On a Tuscan hillside the sculptress Niki de Saint Phalle is at work fabricating the Tarot in enormous, multi-coloured, rotund and topologically complex constructions. She calls herself the Fool, the zero card of the twenty-two of the major arcana. The Magician, card number one, is conceived as a fat serpent undulating his way up over the steps to the entrance, at once mouth and vagina, of the doubly-decked edifice of the High Priestess, card number two, fitting tribute to the pairing of Hank and Tanya, grounded in the plot's prehistory before he took to candy-bars and she to fortune-telling, whose recollection shadowed her throaty murmur over his sodden, floating, bloated corpse. 'He was some kind of man'. The thirteenth, Death, says Mlle de Saint Phalle, is a woman. Gold skinned, large breasted, wearing a onepiece red swimsuit, eye sockets circular in her microcephalous skull, she rides on horseback bearing a bright red scythe with which to mow down all who live in our city and beyond.

The parallel is unmistakable. I, too, am large breasted, with a suntan burnt into my skin except where the shape of a bikini lower half attests to the conventions of a Corfu beach. My fingers feel around the rims of my eye-sockets delving into the skull micrometers beneath the surface. I am certainly not big-headed. And while the Fur Q van is not living flesh it is as temperamental as any thoroughbred steed. But the greatest correspondence between this other woman and myself is in the matter of her scythe and my scissors. With them I cut up my lengths of celluloid just as she cuts down the living, each frame in its rigor mortis a testimony when briefly activated by the projector to the life I stole in the pursuit of my grisly trade. I get like this on bad days.

Mlle de Saint Phalle also says:

'There is no death.

There is change, transformation.

Our life is eternal.'

I ask:

'If death is a woman and there is no death, what then? No death, no woman? Or woman, therefore death? "A Woman? Dead?" Is it a trick? Then who is the trickster? A magician? a fool? F for Faker or Saint Ph-Ph-Phalle?'

Time to consult the Tarot. Method of divination, the Ancient Celtic, in memory of Glasgow. I select the queen of swords, as befits my profession, and place it centre left. Then, from the multiply shuffled and triply cut deck, I deal a second card to be laid across the first, followed by four around them anticlockwise beginning at the bottom, and four more in a column upwards on the right. They designate thus: firstly, the subject, crossed by, secondly, the opposing forces; around them, the material basis, past determinations, present determinations including those of the subject, future determinations; on the right, the subject's fear, the subject's other, the subject's hope, and, lastly, at the top, the outcome. They fall like this,

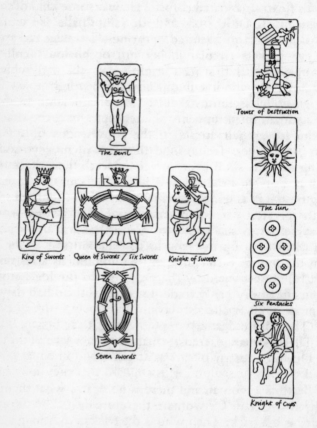

which doesn't look too good to me.

'Though a complete analysis is out of the question, certain indications are called for. We note the exceptional concentration of cards of the same suit as that representing the subject, and, most notably, its being flanked by two cards which precede and follow it in the sequence of the suit. The implications are of an unusual convergence of actuality and the requirements of an ideal or symbolic order. In particular, with the king representing past determinations, and the knight future determinations, there is a perfect transition from paternal to adult heterosexual object choice. We note too the six and seven of swords, summing to thirteen, the subject's key number, thus further confirming her identity, and also showing the opposing forces and material basis of her existence to be intimately linked. Together these two cards comprise a figure whose number within the major arcana signals death, which according to the subject's mythology, private or public, is heralded as a woman. Present determinations are indicated by the devil, libidinally active and unconstrained by the exigencies of the symbolic, which, located as surmounting both the subject and the composite figured death, suggests an unprecedented release of sexually invested death drive. The repetition of the knight and the six on the right also marks the compulsion to repeat characteristic of the death drive. The subject's hopes, represented by the sun, for unity and eros are dashed by the outcome, the tower of destruction, bringing with it fragmentation and chaos. However, the terminus of personality and culture so implied is not without redemption, as is suggested by the alternative name for the card, the house of God. It may be supposed that the resting place of the death drive is ultimately in the peace of absolute non-being, the Nirvana which saints and sages have sought since time began. These bare indications are offered in complete ignorance of the subject's identity, history or circumstances, and in equal ignorance of cinema or sculpture. It is hoped that they may be of some help.'

Molly understood that she must act. A creation herself, she must also create. Hardly a day passed without her thinking about the old man whose dying strength had been poured into her coral reef with its abundance of life – submarine, brilliant, implacable, mysterious. She wanted to do something that would make a difference. After months of indecision it came to her. She too would become a tattooist. She would carry on the art the old man practised. But because she was a woman her art would be different from his. She negotiated an apprenticeship with a tattooist of repute in a city to the south of ours. A year later he disclosed that she had nothing more to learn from him, and she returned north with her scratcher and pigments to set up in business. The premises she found to rent were in the same district, close by one of the two railway termini, as the old man's studio. The previous renter of the large room divided into two by a glass partition had been an exotic importer, and the place still smelt pleasantly of spice. Molly ordered Venetian blinds for the partition, so as to make the inner studio as private as might be required, repainted the woodwork and the walls in two shades of yellow, and furnished it with astute purchases from public auctions, of which the prize was a worn leather psychoanalyst's couch. On this, she decided, her customers would bare their bodies as Freud's patients had once bared their souls. For publicity she had cards printed and distributed in likely places – Chinatown, the docks, the country jail, educational establishments, wealthy suburbs. They looked like this

REDEMPTION TATTOOS

Reparation Restoration Restitution
Anytime   Anywhere

—◦—◦—◦—

MOLLY MOLLOY
13 Terminus Arcade

It soon became clear there was a demand for what she was offering. As she explained to the many callers, she would only supplement existing tattoos, not originate them. Her work was designed for people whose tattoos had ceased to please them. Since removal was never completely successful, the better alternative for sufferers was to add to what was already there and so change its meaning. If in time these revisions too became a source of distress, they could be yet further supplemented, ad infinitum. The traces were indelible, she told customers, but the possibilities for re-interpretation were unlimited.

Over the years Molly prospered and her reputation spread. She numbered the rich and powerful among her clientèle, but never turned away anyone in need of her services for want of funds to pay. In due course she was acclaimed as our city's greatest living artist and was given its freedom.

During a globally networked TV programme celebrating fifty years of her practice, she was asked which works she would cite as her outstanding masterpieces.

Molly replied that she felt it was not for her to say whether any of them fell into that particular category, which was not one she used herself, but she would be pleased to speak of seven which, upon mature reflection, best exemplified the nature of her artistic project.

The interviewer said that she herself and the billions watching would feel privileged to hear such a dissertation.

Molly asked if it would be acceptable for her to read from the diary she had kept since she was a tattoo-less girl, in order that the exact flavour of her experience could be rendered.

The interviewer agreed that this would be more than satisfactory.

Molly stressed that the order of the extracts was immaterial and achronological.

The interviewer lowered her gaze and the watching billions concentrated theirs.

Molly read from her diary.

'The girl with the red rose on her arm who walks by the canal came to me today. Her name is Polly. She told me that she feels so ravaged by the demands of her profession that her rose should be obliterated. She wanted it blackened as if by fire or blight. I remonstrated that her own beauty

177

deserved better than that. To mortify her own flesh to absolve the guilt of others would be a tragic waste. I showed her my own body and her eyes lit up majestically. We talked about alternatives, ways to preserve yet modify the compromised rose. One idea was to turn her into an alpine pasture, until the story we concocted to justify the presence of the rose among the gentians and edelweiss, one involving a skier who had discarded it on the wintry slopes, his overnight drive in a BMW to beg forgiveness, and a happy ending on the Côte d'Azur, made it ludicrous. Out of our shared laughter I associated freely and from skier got flyer and from flyer got an image of a glossy green beetle hovering above and a little to the left of the rose. In the book of insects on my shelf I found it. A rose chafer, *Cetonia aurata*. Polly was delighted. I used a metallized emerald pigment to get the sheen of its wingcases. The chafer now dances attendance on the rose, their two colours achieving a precarious complementarity. As she was leaving Polly speculated on whether her rose chafer would lead to pollination. A Polly nation, I felt bound to quip.'

Yes.

'A very old man, who had been born in a Nazi death camp, came to me today and rolled up his sleeve. "I have carried this number all my life, that I and others should never forget. Now, before I die, I wish to expunge it. Not through any technique that would eliminate it, but through a superabundance in which it will be lost. It will become just one grain of sand upon a beach. I wish to be covered, from head to toe, in one mighty number. *This* number", indicating with a nod, "in becoming just six consecutive digits within the greater number will be relieved of the weight of evil it has borne until now. Yet at the same time the greater number will be what it is through the presence of that part within its whole. That is inescapable. Are you ready to begin?" So we set to work, and the work will take a week, using a randomization algorithm on my pocket calculator. Already the arm which bore the sign of his absolute subjection is a mass of digits. The complete number, when it is written, will never be spoken, will remain blessedly silent.'

Yes.

'For reasons she wouldn't divulge the customer had the

Southern Cross and Orion's Belt tattooed on her left and right eyelids. She wished to supplement them with the whole night skies of the southern and northern hemispheres. I agreed to do what she wished, but warned her that the micro-needling technique that I must use would be extremely slow and that during the hours of its implementation she must remain quite motionless. She agreed and I have done it. Each star, planet, nebula is accurately rendered. Now, when she closes her eyes, the visible universe falls like a curtain over her sight.'

Yes.

'She explained, "I was the female half of a magic double act. One day the sawing-in-half routine went terribly wrong. This was the result." Lifting her sweater she showed me the scar. To my amazement it encircled her entire waist. "Some slip-up, uh? I know it's not a tattoo, but can you do anything about it?" I gestured towards the pigment-stained couch. What did she have in mind? She wanted a tattooed belt of a 35mm strip of celluloid with the sprocket holes exactly fitting the line of suture where they'd stitched her back together. Any particular piece of film? It was to be the final sequence of Stella Dallas, when Barbara Stanwyck in the title role turns from the window through which she has been watching her daughter's marriage and walks away down the street tragic yet exultant.'

Yes.

'No pretext, a compassionate exception to my rule. She came to me, this woman, in desperation. It became apparent she was suffering a bereavement, possibly a child. She spoke of two Madonnas by Bellini, one hanging in Glasgow, the other in São Paolo, copies of which are to be found in our city's gallery. We went, she and I, to the Renaissance salon and breathed in the sacred air of Bellini's motherhood. In the first, Mary looks absently away from the infant Jesus who dangles a flower on a thread above her upturned palm; in the second, she looks sidelong at the child whose hands encircle her neck in a strangler's grip. "I want the madonna's two faces to be superimposed upon my own, in such a way that you see the one from the one side and the other from the other, and never both simultaneously. I would like a child at each breast, the little lover on the left, the little murderer on the right." If it could be done, I would do it, I told her. Stereo tattooing, using a polarizing laser scratcher, has been recently perfected in the Soviet Union, though the Party disapproves. My phonecall to a comrade on the shores of Lake Baikal gave me the information I needed. I set to work last weekend, with the two kindly loaned paintings tacked up on the wall. Today we finished, and the results are astonishing. She declared, with tears coursing down her faces, that she felt entire once again. After she had gone I removed my blouse and stared in the mirror at the Siamese fighting fish, *Betta splendens*, upon my own breast. I felt giddy with a surge of incompatible emotions.'

Yes.

'The customer phoned beforehand to make an appointment, insisting upon complete privacy and confidentiality. On arrival he asked whether the "Anywhere" on my business card meant *anywhere*. I could tell he was a banker by the indescribable odour of money exuding from him. Anywhere, I said. This, he said, unzipping trousers, dropping underpants, could I do anything. The banker's penis was stippled with the unmistakable colouration of tattoo, but what it represented was hidden by his detumescence. I told him to relax and transform himself into a condition of visibility. With foreskin retracted, glans engorged, and the shaft elongated up over his belly, the nature of the representation became evident. I admired the craftsmaship. Erectile tissue is a notoriously difficult medium to work. The glans itself was toned around its natural shape to represent a Nazi military helmet. Beneath it, tattooed on the rampant underside of the penis, there was a skull now properly proportioned by his erection to stare sightlessly at whoever or whatever was the object of his lust. The remainder of the shaft portrayed a ballistic missile, with three of the four visible tailfins bearing the signs $, £ and F. He had come to me, he said, as a last resort. If I couldn't help, well, he couldn't answer for the consequences. I insisted first of all he tell me how he had acquired the tattoo. His rambling story, embellished by self-justificatory romanticization, boiled down to this: he had been taken captive in a country in the southern hemisphere whose newly independent government was fighting for its survival against a nearby racist state which was taking his loans to finance a covert war by I-LID; he had been handed over to a group of peasant women whose children had been murdered in a pacification raid; the tattoo had been their comment on his existence; he had been released after a ransom of $100,000 had been paid. I asked him what proportion of his personal wealth this represented. Point one of one percent, maybe, was his reply. I told him that I and only I could help him, and would on one condition. Which was? he asked. That he produce evidence to show that he had transferred the other 99.9% to those whose struggle for life his money had opposed. I figured if we got 1% we'd be doing all right. A week later he was back with affidavits, signatures, bankers' drafts and the other paraphernalia of his change of heart. Very well, I said, but before I set to work he must hear me out. "You see the flying fish upon my face? The symbol of freedom and joy skimming across the waves. But the reason the flying fish flies is not carefree enjoyment of life, it is terror, using the adaptation that allows it to escape the barracuda hunting it beneath the surface. *Exocetus volitans*. It has a weapon of destruction named after it. With this in mind I now propose my re-interpretation." The addition to his tattoo, which I began three days ago and finished late tonight comprises a vine, gloriously luxuriant and covering his entire body (save the face – such are the protocols of banking) with a proliferation of leaf and fruit. Its roots reach down into the abandoned, recycled, soil-filled, well-manured containers of helmet, skull and missile cylinder. Given the context the emblems of death can become the material of life.'

Yes.

'She bore the most wonderful whole body tattoo I have ever seen. A classical Chinese landscape with lakes, waterfalls, mountains, trees in blossom, through which deer wandered and birds flew and people discoursed, traded, made love. I asked what more she could possibly want. "Writing", she replied, "I want an inscription to wind from my forehead where the distant peaks of Shensi province reach heavenwards down to my feet where peasants draw water from the wells of my home province of Sichuan. If I write the characters, will you transcribe them to my body?" So with enviable ease she calligraphed the ideograms on paper with a soft brush, while I painstakingly reproduced them in the spaces on her skin where the images shaded into ground. Their meaning I did not know and did not ask, and she did not tell me. I found their forms very beautiful. When it was done the woman thanked me and left as silently as she had arrived.'

Twelve

Gropius the changeling threads his passage through the darkness waving his ticket in the flashlight beam, hands over a buck to the doe-eyed usherette, merci m'sieur, settles himself one third of the way back from the screen. From his pocket he takes a tomato sandwich and eats it. Music, a Satie Gnossienne, can't say where it's coming from, envelops us. Tonight's bag of avant-garde has in it Brakhage's He Was Born, He Suffered, He Died, nine minutes of coloured leader interpolated by black, that Joyce Chan, seated diagonally behind him, finds insufferably tedious, but I concede that others, by which I mean the spare figure silhouetted against the frame to my right, may be enraptured by it. A glance at Gropius from the virtual field of the film finds his face tear-runnelled through the stubble. Something's gotten to him. Could be pure mechanism, to do with brain waves and optics, though he as a card-carrying Jungian, membership in his wallet, would scorn such an attempt to reduce. Can life's pain be nullified by the administration of ever-increasing doses of soma? Anyhow, whatever's witnessing his passion is inclined to take pity on him, more than he deserves. There's talk of a trade-off, his life for his money, a restitution of grace where only death might be supposed to hold dominion. The reprieve is provisional. . . on good behaviour? Or good behaviourism, grumbles the usherette prodding a customer until she coughs up the customary tip.

Hand in pocket, Gropius is generating, reflexively, a hexagram, each line of which is so charged as to be changing into its opposite. Against the odds then, hexagram 64, Before Completion, 未濟 the last of the Book of Changes, becomes 63, After Completion, 既濟 the penultimate. The details don't matter, though students of the particular will note the set of correspondences between the text of the lines and the circumtext where Gropius has figured. The transitions are to do with equilibria, stable and unstable. The text of the changing line at the top reads:

> There is a drinking of wine
> In genuine confidence. No blame.
> But if one wets his head,
> He loses it, in truth.

The conditional implies it is touch and go for Gropius. Termini beckon enticingly. Without access to his mentation the question he has put to the oracle remains open. In place of which, consider an objective correlative for this global instant he exists within, the movements of his six women.

Polly's on a plane about to land at the airport, after a month on a yacht in the Aegean with an aging, but still vigorous Greek. Sara is thinking, a full day once a month doing nothing else, with our city spread out before her from the heights of her appartment. Marie-Fidèle is in bed with the barkeep from the snooker club, teaching him the rudiments of French pillow-talk. Clemency is serving up roast lamb fragrant with rosemary, a gesture of reconciliation towards Gerald, who's been rather nice to her recently. Pru's looking for a parking space near the library, some books to return, in a hurry to get there before it closes. And the sixth?

Joyce Chan, recognizing Gropius from somewhere, I can't think where though, smiles a greeting when the lights go up. They share a bottle of wine in the foyer bar, synchronize body language and inner speech over recollections of liked/disliked films, leave bonded.

That's all folks? A happy ending? Not yet it's not.

For Gropius enters, as they exit on to the street, a condition of undecidability, not unlike that ascribed to the so-called virtual particles associated with the weak nuclear force which cannot be comprehended within a binary logic of existence or non-existence. At the same time Joyce's grandmother, in the hills of Sichuan, takes a bundle of dried yarrow stalks, unties their silk ribbon, runs them through her fingers, their levity sensitive to the lightest touch of breeze lifting the leaves of the willow she sits beneath. The I Ching, still working after several millenia, more than I can say for my spin dryer, is the index of his condition. He suggests something to eat, and I suggest my uncle's restaurant, where they've got this way of doing carp you'll not believe. The period allotted to virtual particles is very short, they've got to squeeze through the temporal gate allowed by relativistic quantum effects. The top line is where the crunch comes. Undecidability is a concession, not a right, and Gropius is going to have to re-enter the world of actuality. The options on offer: tea they'll constantly replenish, or brandy. He drinks the whole half bottle, Joyce couldn't stop him, and staggering through our city's wet reflecting street challenges the bus, in a gesture of unconscious solidarity, that had once slain Adolphus' mother, but the brakes slammed on hard by the driver have on them a slick of oil, and in an amazing series of shot/reverse shots between Gropius' enlarging terrified face, a nice face, and the enlarging indifferent radiator grille, which we know is a quote from the climax of NNW's crop-dusting sequence, his last nanoseconds tick away, until splat!, flattened by the sixth wheel of the double decker, he dies. Alternatively, with the lightest touch I run my forefinger over the standing hairs of his wrist, and say, Why not have tea? Why not? he says, and does. No bus, no terminus. It's not the end at all, there's more to come.

Thirteen

Nothing happened – no smoke pouring forth from fused circuitry, no compression waves rupturing eardrums, no klaxons blaring for the imminent end of civilization as we know it. This was the bathos of the button.

But wait. All was not as it had been. I sensed another shift of genre. I say I, the dubiety not solely of a soulless simulacrum, more serious yet. Where there had been one there were three, where I, we. I'd call it a weepie, the all too familiar litany of fractured females, illness, locked rooms, stairways, maternal sacrifice, except for respect for my cat who hates puns. So I'll make it an art movie. We three then, elementary particles forced apart by the energy pulse of ANNA, stretched into separation along taut elastic bonds, all the elaborate thirdness of quarkdom, had our own ideas of what to do next. Two of us stayed together, the third went my way. The story of the one first, then that of the others.

I felt something brush against my leg. I let out a cry of horror and leapt a yard, but it was still there, rubbing up against me. It was, when I could bring myself to look, Adolphus, alive, bloody and, except for a short section clipped off his tail, entire. Between us we'd survived death's fusillade, though I still couldn't imagine what had come between me and summary extinction out there on the hillside with no replicant to become. I hugged Amadeus to me, noting he smelt like he'd been copulating, the opportunist. Joyful as our reunion was, we couldn't stay there for ever. I had a case to crack, a figure to trace. I saw there was a bell-jar of iced water against one wall, so we'd at least not suffer the torments of thirst on our journey. As I gulped and Augustus lapped from plastic cups, I remembered I still had the tin of sardines I'd picked up from the Fur Q vehicle. I reached into my jacket pocket and, in an instant of pure illumination, understood that this, in its utter contingency, fish netted in the Atlantic, canned in Morocco, sold in Tesco, had saved my life. A miracle. The five little fish, I saw as I unwound the lid with the key, had taken the impact of the bullet and were no no more than a mess of flesh in oil, unaesthetic but still nutritious.

Fortified we set out, across the vacant expanse of the command bunker, into the branching network of corridors leading from it. Adolphus, who I trusted to find his way home, pushed on ahead, down even narrower passages, lit only by flickering candles. Eventually they were devoid of all traces of human construction, just winding tunnels through the encompassing rock, with occasional brightness from patches of phosphorescence. Often I was forced to crawl and for one long stretch I had to snake my way forward on my belly with only the odd miaow from up ahead to say it wasn't a dead end. Then the passage would widen again into caverns whose roofs were just a distant echo from high above. We began to climb steadily, and the temperature rose. Throughout our journey, despite the darkness and the constriction, I was curiously devoid of fear. We must have covered miles and I had lost all track of time. Then, suddenly, following a level stretch, I tripped oversomething at my feet. Stooping to investigate I found it was a step, hewn out of the rock. Above it was another, then another. Going up I counted three flights of thirteen. You didn't have to be a movie buff to spot the reference. At least it confirmed my diagnosis as to genre. But that's UCLA filmschool graduates for you.

At the top of the third flight Adolphus sat waiting. He could go no further. Above us was an iron circle, sectioned into eight, which I immediately realized must be one of the entrances set at intervals into the streets of our divided city, giving access to the sewers beneath. I just hoped it wasn't in the Russian zone. I pushed with all my strength and managed to raise one of the heavy flaps. I climbed out, preceded by my cat. We were in Chinatown and it was night.

I felt okay. The krypton-lit streets were crowded. A police lieutenant stood by his prowl car, its rotating blue light throwing expressionist shadows against the walls. He was tapping his nightstick against the palm of his hand and his sergeant was speaking urgently into the radio. An owl hooted, and a cloud sliced open the moon. There was something happening down by the canal. A frogperson wearing a red wetsuit surfaced, holding one end of a rope, which she passed to a knot of men on the bank. I knew what was going to be on the other end of the rope. It was the fat man, shot through the back of the head, one eye blown out, the socket already the refuge for an eel that wriggled briefly across his face before plopping back into the still, oily water. Bloated, grotesque, he was some kind of man and I felt sorry for him. The silence was broken by a peal of manic laughter from a doorway. A black Zil limousine glided past, a face pressed against the smoked glass. I couldn't hang around for the autopsy, there were things that needed doing. For a start, I had to unload Adolphus, my destination being no place for a cat however lucky. I also wanted a change of clothes, three days in denims had me longing for a silk appliqué cheongsam and high, high heels. And, despite a touch of nausea, I wanted to eat. Down the street was a restaurant where I could do all three, Sichuan cooking and a waitress I'd once done a favour for. Adolphus seemed pleased to be reunited with his dad, who'd been adopted by the chef, or at least was reconciled to reconciliation. I ordered frog, spiced eel, wild fennel, green tea, rice, and West Lake soup, then slipped out the back where Lucy Ho said, Sure, take what you like. Dressed to kill, hunger sated, I slid into the odorous, welcoming night and walked the long block to Fêng's.

My other two thirds were there already, waiting.

We had our own complicated route through time and space from the Off Limits room. As we turned to leave, we discovered there was no exit. The way we'd come in was a blank wall, seamless, impermeable. Could this, we wondered, have been ANNA's doing? And if she'd managed to redesign our immediate environment, what other changes might not have been made to the outside world, if ever we reached it? We sat down in the lotus position we'd struggled for so long to achieve back in the Fur Q vehicle, now with no difficulty, and began to meditate upon our circumstances. Fortunately we had tins of sardines in our jacket pockets, for some reason somewhat battered, enough to eke out an existence for a while. And there was a bell jar of iced water in the corner, so at least we'd not suffer the torments of thirst during our internment. Fed, watered, we sat and contemplated the wall.

Gradually, imperceptibly, we noticed that what we'd taken as a uniform grey wall was in fact variegated, a mass of dots of colour which only took on the effect of grey through each being modified by the next. After some time we saw that the dots were not uniformly distributed, but formed whirls and swirls, differentiated patterns, forms, shapes. Much later it became apparent that such patterns could be seen as distinct from a ground, making for discernible marks. After a considerable stretch of time it occurred to us that these marks were the signs of a script, in some unknown language. Later still, we concluded that by selecting certain of these signs we could construct the letters of the Roman alphabet, and then, a while after that, that we could combine them into words. From then it took only a brief moment to find a meaningful sentence.

Assertive, declarative, incontrovertible, it stood before us seated readers even as the wall became a transparent membrane opening out on to landscape, patterned by cloud and evening sunshine to the distant horizon. In our time capsule we had been oblivious to the succession of seasons, years, millenia, aeons, that had eroded the thousands of feet of rock above and lifted us on currents of magma to the very summit of the hills to the east of our city. Now, as this last sedimented stratum was washed away in a late spring squall, we unfolded our limbs from our lotus positions, straightened, stretched, and ran out into the world.

Our momentum carried us forward to the cliff edge, and for me, fractionally in front, digging my heels in on the gravelly domed headland didn't stop me going over. Somehow I managed to grab on to a ledge with my fingertips. It was a cliffhanger and I wasn't up to holding on till the next reel for some man with a nice face to rescue me. No time for that. I looked up and saw me reaching down. I looked down and saw me reaching up. Our fingers met. We hung on and pulled for our life. We took a train into Chinatown. From the station we walked the long block to Fêng's.

Our other third was there already, waiting.

The elastic binding us three over time and space had done its work, bringing us together at our destination. Momentarily we retained our separate identities, appreciative of our differences, then each took a pace towards the others, and we were once more one – and still a knockout in Lucy Ho's dress – a little wiser, a little older, a little thinner, three interlocking yet unlinked rings.

Fêng himself stood in the doorway to greet me. Next to Fêng stood Carrefour, his minder, a 6-foot-6 nigger zombie, naked to the waist, carrying a cocked M16, whose hearing was so sharpened by his sightlessness that he could detect threats to his charge even before their makers had become aware of their own intentions.

'Welcome, Mac Xi-ash. We've not the pleasure of your company for too long. You look well.'

'Thank you, Fêng Hi-lo. I should do, I've got me a new body.'

'It happens to all of us, every seven years, I'm told.'

'You look well yourself. Business must be good.'

'While there are those who are prepared to take a chance I shall not go hungry.'

'And while there are those who go hungry there will always be some prepared to take a chance.'

He and I could go on like this for hours, it runs in the culture, but this time I was taking a raincheck. Evidently sensing my mood, he said, 'Very nicely put. But your destiny awaits. Please follow me.'

Through Fêng's domain we went, with Carrefour unerringly charting the path of least resistance through huddles of representatives of the people cutting for their nations' arms budgets, past roulette wheels where terminally bored bourgeoises languished, over poker tables where house players outnumbered the target bankers by several to one, until we reached the portal of the innermost room. Over the lintel was coiled a painted dragon. From its mouth, in characters of fire, there sprang the ideogram 家人 the family.

Fêng bowed low and gestured for me to enter. 'This is where I leave you. I wish you good fortune.'

Carrefour grinned broadly and put a finger to the side of his nose. I liked Carrefour. He gave the place class. A shame he'd fucked with the voodoo Triads when he was running for mayor. There are some constituents you just can't reason with. I knew I was putting off the moment of entry. I went in.

They were all there, as I'd suspected they would be. An even dozen, the patriarchal number, as non-prime as you can get. A suit filled to the K with no space for the ace. An Augustine calendar, with lunar time eclipsed. A clock chock-a-block, and no time for the thirteenth hour. A 360° compass and no north by northwest. It was a Zodiac snapped by Kodiak and I was out of the picture. It was a jury in a fury and I was the accused. It was a Tupperware supper-party and I was the uninvited guest.

They were ranged around the dice pit, and as I peered dizzingly into it the cloth seemed to be indistinguishable from the fabric of the universe itself. Each of them in turn was rolling the dice, then passing them to her left. I knew them all. In my line of business you get to know who's who in our city, and those I hadn't met before had crossed my path since the late trio had hired me to trace a certain figure. I knew now who was behind the trio. And I knew now that everything I'd gone through had been a series of false leads, a bunch of loose ends, a shoal of red herrings. My sister was one of the twelve, and so was my mother.

My sister said, 'Hullo Anna.'

I moaned, overwhelming by pity for all that had been and was no more, 'Anna's dead. I died beneath the hills to the east of our city. I killed myself.'

My sister repeated, 'Hullo Anna.'

And then I began to understand, slowly at first, but with increasing comprehension. There are two Annas, one who was and one who will be, in an unending ritual of killing under the rule of Chronos for as long as life continues. Sliding imperceptibly from the one to the other, continuous in form and discontinuous in substance, the Anna-to-be becomes the Anna that-has-been. These two thirds bonded indissolubly, were those parts of me that had left the underworld through the agency of time. But what of the remaining third, out through the agency of space? There was more to the story than I'd so far been told, or guessed. Would my sister please fill me in.

'Watch.'

So here come the dice, spilling out across the cloth, tumbling from the hands of the big rollers.

Molly Molloy, our lady of the reef, 1, 6.

Joyce Chan, my sister, mathematician, loved since yesterday by Gropius, 1, 1.

La Jefe, Conchita to her rival, boss of the South side, whose countenance I'd spotted in the limo, 2, 5.

Clemency Black, deep-caver, life-saver, 2, 2.

Polly of the eyes men die for, dice for, 3, 4.

Pru Fell, my mother, showdown winner with a pair of threes, 3, 3.

Persephone Birdwissel, librarian, black cape aflight in the still air, 4, 3.

Marie-Fidèle Persiflage, spellbinder, 4, 4.

The General, who I'll get yet, 5, 2.

Sandra Jewel, 22 carat faker, 5, 5.

Sara Bella, warrior, beauty, 6, 1.

The Professor, the brains of the show, 6, 6.

I still couldn't figure it. So far as I could tell, it just didn't add up. The only way I could read it, my mother with her double three was going to have to make the big sacrifice. But I wasn't having it.

'No momma. You stay where you are. There's no room for a thirteenth.'

My mother, Pru for Prudence, imp for imprudence, with whom my relations have been uneven, gently chided, 'Aren't you forgetting something?'

'I am?'

'Who you are.'

'Who, me?'

'Let Joyce explain.'

I should explain, a bit of family history, that Joyce is my half sister. We share a father, a Shanghai sailor of some charm, who my mother fell for in Glasgow before she moved to our city. He, known as Mac to the roundeyes, repentant, begged her to return, but she, living with her mother, my grandmother, had had enough. He could have the child, he was happy to, raising me in his extensive family, hence my closeness to my baby sister, who always called me Anna, until at fifteen I hit the road. My mother was a visitor, then I was a visitor. I kept in touch but only narrowly. Joyce came to our city to study, stayed on. My grannie died, leaving little but a box of irascible correspondence with Stalin, her own letters painstakingly copied by hand, his clumsily typed on the Kremlin typewriter, a surprise to all of us. I have in-laws in China, though the lineage gets too complex for my westernized mind to comprehend.

Joyce was saying, 'Think back to the whys and the exes.'

I did, all those unanswered questions, half-forgotten lovers, but I still didn't get it.

'Think of two diagonals, intersecting. They form a cross.'

I thought of a cross, and I thought of a doublecross. There were plenty of precedents, and you didn't need to go further than Chinatown to find one.

My mother placed her hands on my shoulders, held me at arm's length, fixing me with her gaze. 'You're suspicious. You must trust us. You must trust yourself. Then you will remember.'

Joyce continued, 'From the point of intersection there extends a line winding outwards. It has the appearance of a web.'

My mother said, 'And you, my natural daughter, are at the centre of it, some way from the origin, in the here and now, spinning the yarn. Each one of us twelve is bound to you by it.'

'And beyond us, countless more, stretching away in time and space.'

My mother pulled me towards her, embraced me. 'The name I gave you is Ariadne'.

And then I began to remember. The knot was loosening. The third third fell into place. Haltingly I recited, 'I am Ariadne. Sometimes known as Arachne, the spider, the thirteenth sign of the Zodiac, between Gemini and Taurus, attribute psychic powers, forgotten at the onset of the modern age, from whose body comes the thread to weave the web that's coeval and co-extensive with the world.'

Around me they were taking their positions.

My mother said, 'We needed to bring you to us. Your route was winding. But you got here in the end.'

I understood it now. I was the figure I'd been hired to trace. Number thirteen. The missing woman. A circuitous route right enough, if I thought back to the arrival of the ill-fated trio at the Fur Q vehicle three days ago. And thinking of that, there were some corpses that needed some explaining too. The lady in the red wetsuit hadn't been exactly idle. This lot weren't averse to cracking osprey eggs to make their omelette. Holy mackerel, it had only been the sardines that had saved my bacon. (Pork haunts me yet.) Not to mention a severed head and a replication I wasn't exactly at home with. Nor a certain person being inveigled into pressing a certain button that could have meant the end of all narratives, big or small.

The twelve are ranged along the diagonals extending from my arms and legs. I sense the power coursing through the figure we form, and the figure turns on me. There's a lot to be done. For a start a few changes need to be made around here. The General, vengeance is sweet, is due for retirement, and while I'm at it, La Jefe too. Their granddaughers, two more Annas, no names are unique, are eager to take their places. Then we'll get going. What a movie we'll make. Maybe first of all I'll do something about Carrefour, no slouch undead, he should be something else alive, more than compensation for Mex and Booris, having trouble with their visas. Perhaps he and I shall found a dynasty together. If I'm as good as my original, I should be good for babies. In any case it could be fun trying. And the kid will get a better deal in the remake, nobody deserves to go like that in the opening scene even if the thirteenth part is required for the plot. There's plenty of time. There's not much time. The thread runs from me tirelessly. Will it stay unspun or become silk cloth? Will it catch rose chafers or clothe my sister? Will it grip Gropius or will it enfold my mother in thick rich textures as she lies awake, late, reading?

MORE CARCANET FICTION

Sebastian Barry	*The Engine of Owl-Light*	0 85635 704 9
Emmanuel Bove	*Armand*	0 85635 639 5
Christine Brooke-Rose	*Xorandor*	0 85635 655 7
Dino Buzzati	*A Love Affair*	0 85635 586 0
Denis Hirson	*The House Next Door to Africa*	0 85635 720 0
Stuart Hood	*A Storm from Paradise*	0 85635 582 8
Peter Hoyle	*Brantwood*	0 85635 637 9
Gabriel Josipovici	*Contre-Jour*	0 85635 641 7
Djanet Lachmet	*Lallia*	0 85635 563 1
Clarice Lispector	*The Hour of the Star*	0 85635 626 3
Pier Paolo Pasolini	*A Violent Life*	0 85635 587 9
Umberto Saba	*Ernesto*	0 85635 559 3
Leonardo Sciascia	*Sicilian Uncles*	0 85635 555 0

For a catalogue describing these and other books on the Carcanet list, write to: Carcanet Press, 208–212 Corn Exchange Buildings, Manchester M4 3BQ, or: Carcanet, 198 Sixth Avenue, New York, New York 10013.

Fiction in Paladin

The Businessman: A Tale of Terror   £2.95   □
Thomas M. Disch
'Each of the sixty short chapters of THE BUSINESSMAN is a *tour de force* of polished, distanced, sly narrative art . . . always the vision of America stays with us: melancholic, subversive and perfectly put . . . In this vision lies the terror of THE BUSINESSMAN'
Times Literary Supplement

'An entertaining nightmare out of Thomas Berger and Stephen King'
Time

Filthy English   £2.95   □
Jonathan Meades
'Incest and lily-boys, loose livers and ruched red anal compulsives, rape, murder and literary looting . . . Meades tosses off quips, cracks and crossword clues, stirs up the smut and stuffs in the erudition, pokes you in the ribs and prods you in the kidneys (as in Renal, home of Irene and Albert) . . . a delicious treat (full of fruit and nuts) for the vile and filthy mind to savour'
Time Out

Dancing with Mermaids   £2.95   □
Miles Gibson
'An excellent, imaginative comic tale . . . an original and wholly entertaining fiction . . . extremely funny and curiously touching'
Cosmopolitan

'The impact of the early Ian McEwan or Martin Amis, electrifying, a dazzler'
Financial Times

'It is as if Milk Wood had burst forth with those obscene-looking blossoms one finds in sweaty tropical palm houses . . . murder and mayhem decked out in fantastic and erotic prose'
The Times

To order direct from the publisher just tick the titles you want and fill in the order form.

Original Fiction in Paladin

Paper Thin   £2.95   ☐
Philip First
From the author of THE GREAT PERVADER: a wonderfully original
collection of stories about madness, love, passion, violence, sex and
humour.

Don Quixote   £2.95   ☐
Kathy Acker
From the author of BLOOD AND GUTS IN HIGH SCHOOL: a
visionary collage–novel in which Don Quixote is a woman on an
intractable quest; a late twentieth-century LEVIATHAN; a stingingly
powerful and definitely unique novel.

To order direct from the publisher just tick the titles you want
and fill in the order form.

Fiction in Paladin

In the Shadow of the Wind   £2.95 □
Anne Hébert
Winner of the Prix Femina
'A bewitching and savage novel . . . there is constant magic in it'
Le Matin

'Beautifully written with great simplicity and originality . . . an
unusual and haunting novel'
London Standard

Love is a Durable Fire   £2.95 □
Brian Burland
'Burland has the power to evoke time and place with total authority
. . . compelling . . . the stuff of which real literature is made'
Irish Times

To order direct from the publisher just tick the titles you want
and fill in the order form.

All these books are available at your local bookshop or newsagent, or can be ordered direct from the publisher.

To order direct from the publishers just tick the titles you want and fill in the form below.

Name _____

Address _____

Send to:
Paladin Cash Sales
PO Box 11, Falmouth, Cornwall TR10 9EN.

Please enclose remittance to the value of the cover price plus:

UK 60p for the first book, 25p for the second book plus 15p per copy for each additional book ordered to a maximum charge of £1.90.

BFPO 60p for the first book, 25p for the second book plus 15p per copy for the next 7 books, thereafter 9p per book.

Overseas including Eire £1.25 for the first book, 75p for second book and 28p for each additional book.

Paladin Books reserve the right to show new retail prices on covers, which may differ from those previously advertised in the text or elsewhere.